Traveling Circus

Story and Illustrations by
Ingar Rudholm

Ingar Rudholm

Thanks to my mom for teaching me how to draw
and to my dad for encouraging me to write.

Acknowledgments

~

Thanks, Uncle Donald Ingersoll, for providing words of wisdom and encouragement. You took a rough draft, polished it, and turned it into something special.

1

The leaves on the trees were turning in the small town of Whitehall on that mild autumn evening. The scent of elephant ears, French fries, and roasted peanuts drifted away as the upbeat music and cheerful laughter subsided. The lights on the amusement rides flickered, prompting the herd of carnival-goers to slowly shuffle toward the exit.

Flynn Parkes knew he needed to rush home soon to avoid getting into trouble with his parents for having snuck out of the house. Without bumping into anyone, he weaved his thin clumsy body through the crowd. His blue squinty eyes fell upon Rena Gainsborough, a girl from his ninth-grade art class. Flynn scratched his blond hair as he watched Rena, her twin sister Deana, and their parents walk into the main circus tent with the ringmaster. The sight sparked Flynn's curiosity. Without making a conscious decision to do so, he turned and followed the Gainsboroughs against the flow of the crowd. Little did he know that his life would never be the same.

Flynn hid behind a rhinoceros that was being led toward a cage by a trainer. As the rhino and trainer passed the main tent, Flynn snuck inside the tent and ducked underneath the wooden bleachers. He gazed up at a brown canvas roof supported by ropes and poles. In the center of the tent, he saw three circular stages lit by a chain of overhead lights. From under the bleachers, he overheard Rena's dad haggling with the ringmaster.

"Salvatore, you keep bragging about a private show. But how much does it cost?" Mr. Gainsborough asked skeptically.

"It's absolutely priceless!" Salvatore exclaimed.

Mr. Gainsborough, a stout man with thinning hair, was the wealthy owner of a construction company. When it came to his two daughters' happiness, money was no object. Deana enjoyed her father's generosity by asking him to buy her fancy clothes, expensive jewelry, and designer shoes. Rena, on the other hand, didn't wear pink or the latest style. She had three rules when it came to clothes: comfort, casual, and no-nonsense. Unlike Deanna, Rena wasn't worried about impressing the "popular" or "pretty" kids in school.

"When the show is over, you can pay me whatever you choose." Salvatore bargained. "What do you have to lose?"

Mr. Gainsborough agreed to Salvatore's unusual offer, and the family took a seat in the front row.

The lights dimmed, and a spotlight shone down on Salvatore as he moved to the edge of the center ring. He had brown hair and a thin mustache that curled up on each side in half circles. He appeared to be in his late forties and wore a long black coat.

Picking up a microphone, he announced grandly, "For the first act, let me introduce Sammy the clown!"

The spotlight then swept across the floor, climbed up a trapeze ladder, and landed on a platform. On it stood Sammy, a clown wearing a gold jester's hat, gold pants, vest, and gloves that extended just above his elbows. His chin was painted white, and he had a white star on his cheek. He twirled a rope over his head like a cowboy lasso and then threw the looped end into the air.

Flynn wondered what Sammy was trying to catch since nothing was there. Before he could venture a guess, the rope froze in place like a movie on pause. Flynn rubbed his eyes. He struggled to figure out how he did that magic trick.

Sammy tied the end of the rope to the trapeze ladder and walked confidently onto the rope. When he reached the center, he slid his hand into his pocket, pulled out three gold balls, and proceeded to juggle them.

Astonished, Flynn glanced over at Rena and Salvatore.

Rena's brown eyes widened as she asked, "How does he do that?"

"Young lady, everything you see inside this tent is an illusion, your imagination, or something else." Salvatore winked mischievously.

Salvatore placed a pocket watch into his pocket, strolled over to a star-covered box, opened the lid, and pulled out a bicycle pump.

As Sammy walked back onto the platform, the rope went limp. He untied the end from trapeze ladder, and the rope dropped to the floor. After climbing down the ladder, he stood next to the rope, and Salvatore handed him the bicycle pump. Sammy placed the mouth of the air hose to the end of the rope, and as he pumped, air magically filled the rope, turning it into the shape of a long cylindrical balloon.

Flynn heard the balloon squeak as Sammy pinched, rolled, and twisted it into the shape of a person. The balloon floated above the ground for a moment. Slowly, it transformed into Sammy's identical twin, except the twin's vest and gloves were reddish-brown instead of gold.

"Let me introduce you to Buster the clown!" Salvatore exclaimed, waving his arms like a showman.

Flynn felt like he was in a dream, and he stretched his mind to understand. *How can a rope turn into a balloon, and then into a man?* Everything at this circus seemed impossible to fathom.

Sammy and Buster took a bow and then disappeared behind a curtain.

"For the next act, we'll need the assistance of Jack, our animal trainer," Salvatore announced.

Jack walked into the tent with a short whip in one hand and the reins of a rhinoceros in the other. He was a medium built man dressed in tan cargo pants, a brown leather vest, and a fedora hat. He led the hefty rhino to the third ring and fed it some leaves, and then the animal sat down.

The lights dimmed, and Salvatore said in a grandiose voice, "Prepare to be amazed by the power of Marcel the Champ!" Salvatore pulled back the flap on the entrance, and Marcel strode to the third ring.

Flynn's jaw dropped.

Marcel's gigantic shorts were the size of blankets sown together; his fists were the size of boulders and his legs looked like tree trunks. His muscles bulged from all parts of his body. Flynn thought giants were a myth, people that only existed in fairy tales.

Marcel bent down, placed his hand under the rhinoceros's belly, and picked the animal up like dumbbells. He did a couple arm curls with the enormous creature as if it were as light as a balloon.

"Marcel is the strongest man in the world!" Salvatore bragged.

With its feet dangling in the air, the rhino squirmed uncomfortably in Marcel's hand while letting out a low grunt. Marcel gently set the animal on the ground.

Rena, Deana, and her parents clapped in amazement as Jack pulled the reins and cracked a whip to guide the animal out of the tent.

Enthralled with the show, Flynn's worries about his parents and his overdue homework vanished like mist into thin air.

Sammy and Buster re-entered the tent pushing two cannons to the stage farthest away from Marcel. A man and a woman, both dressed in white jumpsuits, helmets, and boots, walked behind the clowns. Once in position, Buster loaded the cannons with gunpowder while the couple climbed inside the barrels.

"Where's the safety net?" Rena asked Salvatore.

Flynn was wondering the same thing.

"Rego and Paula don't need nets," Salvatore responded smugly and waved at Buster to proceed.

Buster lit the cannons' fuses with a lighter.

KABOOM!

The cannons' explosion shook the tent and thrust Rego and Paula into the air. They spread their arms out in unison, and with lightning speed, they flew past Marcel. Before slamming into the tent wall, white-feathered wings sprouted from their shoulder blades and the couple swooped upward in an arc. Like graceful swans, they performed a synchronized ballet. Diving above the bleachers, Paula skimmed over Rena's head close enough to rustle her black pixie haircut. Then, they circled around the bleachers and landed on the center stage. Their wings and feathers disappeared beneath their jumpsuits. Rena, Deana, and her parents sat in the bleachers, awestruck by the show.

Flynn anxiously watched Marcel push the cannons outside. Everyone except Salvatore and Jack left the tent, and the lights were turned on.

"That was amazing!" Mrs. Gainsborough gushed. Normally she was prim and proper, but tonight she had let her guard down. Besides, none of her rich friends were around to judge her behavior.

"I call their performance *sky circus*. If you think that's amazing, wait until you see the final act." Salvatore said, alluding to more surprises.

The lights dimmed and the spotlight shone down on Jack walking to the center stage. He carried two Hula-Hoops as three white bunnies hopped behind him. At first this struck Flynn as silly, but the feeling didn't last long.

"Aww, they're cute," Rena said with a sweet smile.

Mrs. Gainsborough smiled and nodded in agreement.

Salvatore gestured toward Jack and spoke into the microphone, "For the last act, Jack will need a lovely assistant."

Without any prompting, Deana brushed her long black hair with her fingers and rushed to the center stage.

Geez, why does she always want to be the center of attention? Flynn thought as he shook his head. *She's not the prettiest girl in school.*

Jack handed Deana two Hula-Hoops and said, "Hold one in each hand; extend your arms straight out from your body."

With her arms extended, the rabbits hopped over to Deana. One sat in front of her feet while the other two sat in front of the Hula-Hoops.

Jack bent down, petted two of the rabbits, and then he quickly took a stride backward. He snapped his fingers and the rabbits jumped through the hoops in slow motion. While in midair, the rabbit's white fur turned a light brown, their fluffy feet changed into claws, and their teeth became fangs. The rabbits morphed and grew into full size lions! They landed on the ground, turned around, and stalked Deana. She dropped the hoops and pulled her arms close to her chest while Rena and her parents jumped to their feet.

Jack petted the third rabbit and it quickly transformed into a lioness. The lioness swiped her paw at Deana, ripping her designer skirt. Suddenly, it jumped on top of Deana, pinned her to the ground, and let out a growl inches from her face.

"Help!" Deana cried, her frightened plea barely escaping her lips.

Flynn stepped back from the bleachers; his heart beat a little faster. *I know Deana is stuck up, but I don't want to see her eaten by lions! What could I do?* He never felt strength in the face of fear.

2

"No!" Mrs. Gainsborough gasped in horror. "Do something!" she screamed at her husband and the ringmaster.

Rena hid behind her father.

Deana sobbed and her body trembled as the other lions circled around her.

"What are you willing to pay for your daughter's safety?" Salvatore asked. His tone had changed to that of a devious criminal.

"I'll pay you anything!" Mr. Gainsborough pleaded. "Just save my daughter!"

"Give me all your wealth," Salvatore said with a greedy smile.

Mr. Gainsborough hesitated to the excessive ultimatum, but his wife quickly agreed to the ringmaster's demand.

Salvatore reached into his jacket, pulled out his gold pocket watch, and raised it to eye level. While looking at the center stage, he rotated his wrist back and forth. A popping sound filled the rafters of the tent while white confetti fell from the ceiling like snowflakes. As the watch swung like a pendulum on a grandfather clock, the confetti slowed down and then stopped in midair as if connected to the ceiling with an invisible string.

The circus act froze in time. Deana's body looked like that of a wax figurine, her face locked in fear, and the lions looked like mounted animals in a hunter's trophy room.

Baffled by the turn of events, Flynn felt trapped inside a nightmare. His shoulders shivered and sweat dripped off his forehead. He wished he'd just awaken safely inside his bedroom. Unsure of what to do next, he stayed hidden underneath the bleachers.

Salvatore coldly turned to the family, swung the pocket watch, and demanded, "Gather all your money, jewelry, and your daughter's fancy clothes. Bring everything back to me by midnight. If you call the police, this will be your daughter's final act."

Falling into a trance, Rena and her parents ran out of the tent, drove home, and gathered their valuables.

Satisfied, Salvatore placed the watch back into his coat pocket.

Flynn's eyes scanned the room for a quick exit. Jack guarded the front entrance and Marcel stood by the rear exit. Flynn quickly turned around and surveyed the tent wall. *Maybe I can slip underneath,* he thought. He pulled up on the canvas, but it was tightly secured to the ground with stakes. He could barely slide his hands underneath it let alone his entire body.

Why didn't I just go home? Flynn cursed his predicament. Fearful that any action would lead him into more danger, he decided to do nothing. *Why am I always trapped in situations I can't escape from?* Flynn wondered. He turned his attention back to Salvatore who paced back and forth on the center stage. Salvatore stopped for a moment when he saw the shiny gold bracelet on Deana's frozen wrist. He unhooked the jewelry and looking pleased with himself, placed it into his pocket.

After what seemed like an eternity, Rena and her parents returned just before midnight with all the valuables and cash they could pull together. Mr. Gainsborough had a check he made out to "Cash" for the entire amount in his bank account. This would enable Salvatore to cash it without any questions.

"That's all I have. I held up my end of the bargain," Mr. Gainsborough pleaded. "Now, let my daughter go!"

Salvatore pawed through the loot they had brought, and he looked satisfied. Tucking the check in his pocket, he commanded his crew to take the rest of the ransom to his motor home and lock it up.

"Pleasure doing business with you," Salvatore sneered.

Salvatore grabbed the pocket watch from his jacket and swung it back and forth. Spellbound, Flynn watched the circus act unfreeze and the white confetti fluttered to the ground. Jack walked up next to the lions and petted each one. The lions quickly morphed back into harmless rabbits.

Deana's suspended face became animated and alive once again. She blinked and looked around. With no lions or danger surrounding her, she ran into her parents' arms where they embraced in a silent hug.

Salvatore turned to the family swinging the pocket watch back and forth. Their eyes widened. Fixating on the watch, they fell into a hypnotic state.

"You'll have no recollection of the past few hours," Salvatore spoke in a monotone voice. "You won't remember or wonder where your money, clothes, or jewelry went. You won't remember your daughter being in any danger. All you'll remember is that you had an amazing time at the circus."

He stopped the pocket watch and snapped his fingers. As if awakening from a deep trance, they rubbed their sleepy eyes and their memories of the last few hours melted away.

A little disoriented, Mr. Gainsborough asked, "Is the show over?"

"Yes," Salvatore answered politely. His tone changed then, and he acted once more like a decent person. "That's the last performance of the night."

With cloudy eyes, Mrs. Gainsborough said, "We had a wonderful time. Thanks for a spectacular show! What do we owe you?"

"Nothing. Just tell your friends how much you enjoyed it," Salvatore said with a sly grin. "We'll be back in town next year. I hope you and your friends stop by for a new show."

"Thank you," Mr. Gainsborough said, still looking a bit foggy. "We'll spread the word."

As the family walked cheerfully out of the main tent, they waved their good-byes. When they were gone, Salvatore barked at his crew, "Pack the equipment and costumes. Another city awaits the Traveling Circus!"

The workers showed their allegiance to Salvatore by dismantling the three circular stages and main tent.

With adrenaline pumping through his veins, Flynn crouched and inched his way between the support posts of the bleachers. As he rounded the end of the bleachers, he saw an opening in the side of the tent. He hoped to take in a breath of free air. Instead, he ran straight into two burly circus employees. They grabbed Flynn's arms and dragged him to Salvatore. Flynn struggled to break free, but their hands were as strong as vice-grips.

"Who are you?" Salvatore asked angrily. "How much have you seen?"

"I promise, I won't tell anyone," Flynn stammered, his words barely audible.

"So you say! What's your name boy?" Salvatore shouted furiously.

"Flynn Parkes," Flynn mumbled as the blood drained from his face. "I won't tell my parents. They don't know I'm here," he said quietly.

Salvatore rubbed his chin. "That solves that dilemma, but it leaves one last problem."

"What problem?" Flynn inquired.

With a finger pointed at Flynn, Salvatore exclaimed, "You saw the greatest show on earth for *free*! No one has done that before."

A knot formed inside Flynn's stomach. *Oh no, he's going to erase my mind!*

"Why don't I keep you around for awhile?" Salvatore suggested his thoughts out loud. "Everything in life has a price. I'll find a job for you. As soon as you pay off your debt to me, I'll release you with no memory of this deal."

"What do you mean?" Flynn shook his head in disbelief. "You can't kidnap me! I promise, I won't tell anyone. Let me go! I have school tomorrow."

Ignoring Flynn's pleas, Salvatore extended his hand and said, "That's my final offer."

Flynn was afraid to shake his hand, so Salvatore grabbed Flynn's hand and shook it.

"A handshake seals the deal," Salvatore declared, pleased that he had found another recruit. "Jack!" Salvatore shouted.

Jack ran from the main entrance of the tent. "Yes sir?"

"Take the kid away and lock him inside the rabbit cage," Salvatore ordered.

"No!" Flynn yelled. He tried to run away, but Salvatore tripped him, and he clumsily fell to the ground.

Jack grabbed Flynn's foot and dragged him out of the tent. Flynn unsuccessfully strained to kick and wiggle himself free. Jack jammed him inside a rusty rabbit cage and locked the door. Flynn was stranded in the middle of the fairgrounds. He was squished and unable to stand up, so he crawled around on his hands and knees, brushing rabbit droppings aside. The rabbits scurried out of the way, making room for their unwelcome guest.

During the struggle, a folded piece of paper had fallen out of Flynn's pocket. He saw it a few feet away from the stinky rabbit cage. The paper had a pencil drawing of Rena on it. Even though they were so close, Rena and the drawing seemed out of reach.

Flynn felt invisible and alone. "Help me!" he yelled out in desperation.

No one, not even the darkness, responded to Flynn's plea. He watched the tents being dismantled and packed inside semitrucks by several workers. They didn't appear to have any special powers yet remained under Salvatore's control. In a short period of time, they had the props, costumes, and personal items loaded into the campers.

Marcel emerged from the darkness, lifted the rabbit cage Flynn was trapped in, and loaded it into a semitruck trailer. As Marcel closed the truck's door, pitch black consumed the trailer.

Fear devoured Flynn's soul when he heard the diesel engine roar to a start. He could smell burning diesel fuel and feel the rabbit cage vibrating as the truck began traveling along a gravel road. His hope faded and his troubles widened with every turn of the truck's wheel.

Flynn rested his head on a bed of straw and wondered how he had gotten into this mess. Before falling asleep to the grumbling drone of the diesel engine, the events of the day replayed in his mind.

3

Earlier that afternoon…

Flynn's blue eyes jumped from Mr. Blake, his English teacher, to the classroom floor, and then to the clock above the whiteboard. Wishing time moved faster, Flynn nervously tapped his foot and pushed his thin fingers through his blond hair. The monochromatic walls and checkered floor didn't calm his nerves.

Deana Gainsborough sat in front of Flynn wearing her designer outfit. While playing with her gold bracelet, she finished reading a passage from *The Catcher in the Rye*.

Dreading his turn to read, Flynn cleared his dry throat, squirmed in his seat, and mumbled a few sentences. He felt like a spotlight was shining on his shoulders as he stumbled over his words.

"I can't hear you. Can you speak a little louder?" a short and plump Mr. Blake requested while adjusting his black necktie.

Flustered even more, Flynn stuttered as he read louder.

"What's wrong with you?" Deana asked mockingly, flipping her long black hair with her hand. "Do you need to go back to special-ed?"

Flynn's face turned bright red as two football players laughed at Deana's joke.

"Knock it off, guys. That's not funny," John protested.

John was Flynn's trusted friend whom he'd known since kindergarten. Over the years, they had hung out after school because they shared the same hobby, drawing comic books. Despite being a star football player with a husky frame and gelled brown hair, John always stuck up for Flynn.

"What are you going to do about it?" Vinnie dared.

Vinnie was the quarterback for the JV football team. He was the exact opposite of Flynn; he looked and acted tough.

"You'll see on the field," John warned.

"Bring it," Ruben, a big lineman on the team, challenged while puffing out his chest.

Ruben spoke with a lisp, an "imperfection" that no one dared mention. He quickly jumped on other people's shortcomings, probably as a way of deflecting attention from his own.

"Whatever," John droned, pretending to be unimpressed.

"Easy guys," Mr. Blake said impatiently. "Save the aggression for football practice." Mr. Blake was also the high school football coach.

When the bell rang, Flynn remained in his seat as his classmates gathered their books and rushed out of the classroom. Flynn felt frustrated by his insecurity and wished he could disappear.

Mr. Blake walked over to Flynn's desk and placed a hand on his shoulder.

"Maybe you could practice reading aloud in front of your parents."

"Maybe," Flynn replied without making eye contact.

Flynn grabbed his books and stood up. His tall thin body towered next to that of his short, stocky teacher. Flynn nodded and left the classroom with his head down.

As Flynn walked down the hall, Vinnie and Ruben shoved him into an open locker door. His books flew out of his hands. His shoulder slammed into the cold metal, sounding like two cymbals clashing together.

"Quitter," Vinnie snickered.

Flynn had played football and was reasonably good, but he had lost interest and quit the team awhile back. Ever since then, Vinnie and Ruben had given Flynn a hard time.

One of these days, I'm going to knock those guys out, Flynn thought.

As he knelt down to pick up his books, he noticed Deana Gainsborough's twin sister Rena out of the corner of his eye. She wore faded blue jeans and black high-top Converse shoes. Her T-shirt had a picture of Albert Einstein with frizzy hair and his tongue sticking out.

Looking concerned, Rena walked over to Flynn and asked, "Are you OK?"

Flynn started to reply, but no words came out of his mouth. Instead, he just nodded and kept his eyes on his books. He scurried to his locker to avoid further embarrassment.

Art, Flynn's favorite subject, was his last class of the day. He hurried to the back of the room and sat at a table next to John. Looking around, he saw Rena sitting at another table with her friends.

Everybody except Flynn had been working on reports about famous artists over the past few weeks. He dreaded giving his report in front of the class, so instead of completing the assignment, he had procrastinated and come to school empty-handed.

"A few of you still need to give your reports," Miss Hopper, a tall middle-aged woman with blond hair, announced as she sat behind a desk. "You're next." She pointed to John.

John picked up his report and lumbered to the whiteboard. He taped two pictures to it and declared, "My report is about the Dutch artist Johannes Vermeer."

He pointed to one of the pictures and said, "This painting shows a woman focused on sewing a piece of lace. It's titled *The Lacemaker*. Vermeer was one of the first artists to use a camera to create paintings. The earliest known camera was called the *camera obscura*."

He fumbled through his notes and pointed to the second picture. "The *camera obscura* was a large wood box with a small lens on one side. Light and color passes through the convex lens, bounces off a mirror, and hits a piece of paper inside the camera where it can be traced with a pencil."

After discussing Vermeer's techniques, John completed his report by saying, "Vermeer is often called the master of light. Unlike other artists who relied on lamps or candles, Vermeer used sunlight to create realistic paintings."

"Thanks, John, for that great report," Miss Hopper said sincerely. "Rena, it's your turn."

Rena gathered her report and walked to the front of the classroom.

"The name of my report is: 'Is space and time relative to the artist?'" Rena announced. "During the Renaissance period, artists drew in three dimensions: height, width, and depth. For hundreds of years, artists created three-dimensional images with a technique called *linear perspective*."

She turned her attention to the class and said, "Let's fast-forward to the Impressionist period and the Surrealist movement. The Impressionists introduced a new concept: time, the fourth dimension. Their idea was that the world is constantly in motion. They painted an impression, or in other words, the fleeting moments of time. Unlike the Impressionists, the Surrealists drew images from their subconscious and dreams."

As Rena talked, Flynn began to sketch her oval face, short black hair, long eyelashes, and big brown eyes on a piece of paper.

"Dude," John whispered. "Why don't you just ask her out?"

"Sure." Flynn shrugged his shoulders. "Pick her up for a date on my stupid bike?"

John chuckled at Flynn's question. "Have your parents drop you off at a movie or bowling."

"Quiet down back there," Miss Hopper yelled, giving them an angry glance.

Flynn and John dropped their heads and avoided eye contact with their teacher.

"Heck no," Flynn whispered. "My parents would make a big deal about it."

Rena took a long pause so she could focus on her presentation. Her face was alive with enthusiasm.

As Rena placed a Salvador Dali picture on the board, Flynn admired her brown eyebrows and smooth jawline so he added these details to his drawing.

Rena took an audible breath and continued, "Since Salvador Dali admired Johannes Vermeer, Dali painted his interpretation of *The Lacemaker*." Rena pointed to another picture on the whiteboard. "Dali used the shape of rhinoceros horns to recreate the image of *The Lacemaker*. After reading books on Albert Einstein, Dali used rhinoceros horns to symbolize exploding atoms in his painting."

She finished her report with, "Einstein's theory of relativity states the speed of light is constant, while space and time are relative to the beholder. This can only mean one thing: art is in the eye of the beholder. Artists draw the world from their own perspective."

Walking back to her seat, Rena glanced down at Flynn's table. He quickly covered the drawing with his hands.

Oh jeez, I hope she didn't see it, Flynn thought. He folded the drawing and stuffed it into his shirt pocket.

"Wow!" Miss Hopper exclaimed. "That was a great report, Rena."

A few more students gave their reports, and then Miss Hopper glanced at the clock.

"We don't have any more time." Miss Hopper stated. "Flynn, you're off the hook today, but tomorrow you'll need to give your report."

He let out a sigh of relief.

The bell rang and everyone packed their things for a quick exit. As Rena walked past Flynn's table, she said, "I'm sure you have a great report."

Flynn's face turned red, and he barely smiled. He struggled to maintain eye contact; unfortunately, he kept glancing at the floor.

After a few awkward moments of silence, she said, "Well, I guess I'll see you tomorrow."

She walked out of the classroom, leaving Flynn alone.

Darn it. Why didn't I say anything? he thought. *I wish I could have a do-over.*

Flynn's hands gathered his art supplies, but his mind drifted into a daydream about an eighth grade-dance. He remembered the gym being decorated with black and white streamers and balloons. He saw a lot of familiar faces, including Rena's. When he heard the DJ play a song he recognized, he mustered the courage to walk onto the dance floor. He had pretended to blend in with the crowd, but he felt alone when no one wanted to dance with him. Feeling invisible and embarrassed, he decided to go home. As he walked toward the gym doors, a smoke machine created a dense fog that washed over his body like a wave. It felt damp on his skin and soaked up all the oxygen, leaving him breathless. Blinded by strobe lights, all he heard was treble and bass pulsating from the DJ's speakers.

For a brief moment, the smoke parted, and to his surprise, Rena stood between him and the doors. Concealed by the fog, she danced close to his body. Without warning, she leaned forward and gave him a quick kiss on his lips. Flynn froze in place with eyes wide open.

Even though a year had passed since the dance, he still remembered his first kiss. He kept the memory safely tucked in his mind. Time never erased his feelings; it only magnified his insecurity and lack of confidence around girls.

Flynn snapped back to reality, walked to his locker, opened it, and grabbed his backpack. He dropped his homework into the bottom. The school day had come to an end, and the pressure was lifted off his shoulder. Or so he thought.

4

~

Flynn lived only a few miles from Whitehall High School, so he rode his bike home everyday instead of riding the bus. He had the bike forever, and it was getting too small for him. He felt awkward on it, but his parents told him it was "adequate" for a teenager.

Whitehall was a small city with a blend of old-fashioned stores that had a hint of nostalgia for traditional architecture. It had a quiet atmosphere where everyone felt at home. There was a movie theater, bowling alley along with a few restaurants and a strip mall on the edge of town near the highway.

On the way to his house, Flynn rode past the football field. He saw Deana Gainsborough and the other cheerleaders rehearsing a new cheer. Vinnie and Ruben were on the sidelines waiting for the coach to call them onto the field. John and his teammates were practicing a play. John stood hunched over behind the quarterback. When Coach Blake blew the whistle, John broke through the defense and ran down the field. The quarterback threw the ball, and John made a circus catch before being tackled far down the field.

"Way to hustle guys," Coach Blake shouted and clapped.

On the sidelines, Vinnie noticed Flynn's bike and mocked it. "Nice ride!"

Deana and her circle of cheerleader friends heard the comment and giggled.

Flynn felt foolish on his small bike. Maybe he could get a job this summer so he could buy a moped.

"And those rims are killer!" Ruben teased.

John became angry when he heard them taunt Flynn, so he broke formation, ran off the field, and tackled Vinnie and Ruben. They began to scuffle, and an irritated Coach Blake had to pull them apart.

"Do you want to run extra laps after practice? Knock it off!" Coach Blake warned them.

The boys stopped fighting, looked at their coach and said, "No sir."

Worried about his friend, Flynn stopped his bike there by the field.

"You OK?" Flynn shouted to John.

John gave him a thumbs-up. After confirming that his buddy was all right, Flynn began pedaling his bike home.

Flynn was an only child and both of his parents worked, so he let himself into the house with his key. He grabbed a soft drink from the refrigerator and headed upstairs to his bedroom. The gray walls were smothered with movie posters and Flynn's drawings. His parents called his room an "organized mess" and constantly asked him to clean it.

Flynn turned on the radio and grabbed some comic books that were hiding underneath his bed. He picked up a pencil and drawing pad and then sprawled out onto his beige carpeted floor. Drawing images from the comic books relaxed his mind after a long day at school.

The minutes flew by, and he was so lost in his drawing that he didn't hear his mother come home. She worked as a cashier at a local retail store. She walked into his room and turned down his radio. Her brown hair was pulled back in a ponytail, and her dress had a *white calico flower* pattern. The only time Flynn ever saw his mother wear makeup was when she went to work.

"How can you listen to that music? It sounds like a chainsaw," she said, turning up her round nose.

Flynn rolled his eyes.

His mom looked down and saw the comic books. With a subtle look of disapproval, she placed her hands on her hips and asked, "Did you finish your homework?"

"Not yet," Flynn replied sullenly. "I was just getting to it."

But she didn't let him off the hook that easily. She walked over to Flynn and grabbed the comic books.

Oh great. Now I can't draw anymore Flynn thought.

"Dinner will be ready in an hour, so start your homework," she commanded as she shut the door behind her.

Flynn pulled out his homework from his backpack and slouched down at his desk. Instead of working on his homework, Flynn's mind wandered. He wondered why he couldn't let the real Flynn out of his cage. He had dreams and desires, but an invisible force that he dared not challenge gripped him like a vice.

After several minutes, Flynn heard a truck pull into the driveway. He slid the curtain back and looked out the window. He saw his dad unload tools from the back of a pick-up truck. A sign on the truck door read "Gainsborough Home Builders"- the construction company owned by Rena's parents. Flynn's dad worked long days and sometimes on the weekends as a carpenter.

"Dinner's ready!" Flynn heard his mother shout.

He went downstairs and joined his mother at the dining room table. Flynn used a spoon to pile a big scoop of mashed potatoes on his plate and stabbed a lamb chop with his fork.

"We're so busy at work," Flynn's dad said when he finally entered the dining room.

He still had sawdust in his hair. He had square shoulders, steely eyes, and calloused hands; he was a rugged man with a firm handshake.

"We finished framing the first floor on a house," Flynn's dad announced. "By Wednesday, we should be done with the second floor. Then, my boss has a big apartment complex lined up for us."

"That's good news, Ray," Flynn's mother said, supporting her husband's hard work. She removed her hairpins and let her hair down.

"Georgia," Ray said as he sat down at the table, placed a hand on his wife's knee, and gave her a kiss. "I'm going to have a busy winter."

"That's cool." Flynn tried to contribute to the conversation even though he had a bored look on his face.

"So, Flynn, how was your day at school?" Georgia turned her attention to her son.

"OK." Flynn shrugged his shoulders.

"Just OK?" Georgia raised her eyebrows. "What did you do?"

"We're reading a book in English class. After dinner, can you help me with..."

"By the way," Ray interrupted Flynn. "Your mother called me and said you were drawing instead of doing your homework." Ray sounded like a prosecutor in a courtroom.

Flynn frowned and set his fork on his napkin. *Oh no, here comes the lecture.*

"You need to focus on your homework instead of art," Ray insisted, crossing his arms and speaking in an authoritative tone. "There's no money in art. I didn't go to college, and look how I've struggled. You need go to college for a business degree."

Flynn looked down at his plate. "I don't know what I should study in college."

"Then learn a trade." Ray started his rant. "You could be a plumber or an electrician."

Flynn sat at the dinner table in silence. He had heard his dad's speech a million times. Instead of arguing, he pretended to listen to his father and wolfed down his meal. Every few minutes, he nodded like a bobble-head toy. Even though he was having dinner with his parents, at that moment he felt alone.

"Flynn!" Ray raised his voice, slammed his fist on the table, and asked, "Are you even listening?"

Flynn's throat turned dry, and he choked on his food. He squirmed in his seat and mumbled a few words.

"I can't hear you," Ray said squarely. "Look me in eyes when I'm talking to you."

Flynn slowly looked up and said, "Yes sir."

After dinner, Ray excused himself from the table and walked into the living room. He needed his "relaxation" time from a hard day at work. Georgia and Flynn were left to clean up the table.

"Can I watch TV?" Flynn asked cautiously, looking at his mother with puppy dog eyes.

"Did you finish your homework?" Georgia crossed her arms.

Darn, he thought, *usually she caves in.*

Looking up at the ceiling, he responded reluctantly, "Nooooo."

"You can watch TV *after* you finish your homework," she said sternly. "But first, take your plate to the dishwasher."

"OK, but can I finish my homework in my bedroom?" Flynn begged as he walked to the kitchen with his plate.

"Yes, I guess." Georgia sighed.

As Flynn climbed the stairs, his shoulders drooped. Ironically, the faint sound of a violin played in the background. After a long day at work and a big dinner, Flynn's father played the violin as a hobby. The sad sound of the violin mocked Flynn's mood. When Flynn closed the door, he felt trapped inside his small bedroom.

Needing some fresh air, Flynn opened the bedroom window and wistfully looked out over the neighborhood. The sun was setting, and the inviting blue sky had turned a rosy aura. The trees' fading leaves reflected the glowing rays of the sun. Flynn contemplated his place in the world. *How did I get here?* he asked himself. He noticed his bike parked by the garage door. *Maybe I'll feel better after a quick bike ride, and then I'll write my art report.* He hesitated for a moment as he thought about whether or not his parents would catch him. *Hmmm, Mom is in the kitchen, and Dad is playing the violin on the opposite side of the house; they can't hear me.*

Without thinking, he walked over to his dresser and grabbed all of the money from a jar that sat on top of it. He climbed out the window and onto the porch roof. From there he stretched out, grabbed the branch of a nearby tree, and climbed down to the ground.

Sensing his freedom, Flynn's feet barely touched the grass as he ran to his bike.

"What could go wrong?" Flynn whispered under his breath; he rode into town with no particular destination in mind.

5

~

Flynn caught a glimpse of a poster nailed to an electric pole. He stopped his bike and read the sign: "One Night Only! A Carnival and Circus in Funnel Field!" The poster ignited his curiosity, so he pedaled his bike in the direction of the park. His mind felt refreshed, and his second wind kicked into high gear.

Flynn saw a long fence surrounding the fairground, and several people were gathered at the entrance. The bike rack was full, so he kept his bike beside him as he walked through the main gate.

Carnival music, shouting, and laughter filled Flynn's ears. The scent of elephant ears, French-fries, popcorn, cotton candy, and roasted peanuts floated through the air. He saw carnival rides to his right and food carts to his left. Straight ahead, he saw several tents. Vendors, musicians, and jugglers were entertaining the crowd. He strolled by a tall Ferris wheel, a rickety old roller coaster, and a Tilt-A-Whirl. As he weaved through the crowd, he read some of the signs on the smaller tents.

"Come See Sammy and Buster the Magic Clowns for $1!" one sign read.

At another tent, he heard a barker call out, "Witness the incredible strength of Marcel the Champ! For two dollars, see him lift eight hundred pounds!"

Moving on, he noticed a huge painting of a beautiful mermaid. The billboard read, "Straight From the Ocean, Come See Cordelia the MERMAID!"

Flynn leaned his bike against the mermaid tent and stepped up to the ticket booth. He handed the attendant six quarters and walked inside with several other customers. He saw a beam of light from the center of the tent where a single bulb dangled from the ceiling. A man stood on a wooden barrel. His nametag read "Salvatore the Ringmaster".

"Witness the beautiful and coy Cordelia." Salvatore held up a microphone and gave his well-rehearsed pitch. "She lives in two worlds—by day she walks on land, and by night she swims in the ocean. Cursed by a spell, her long legs turn into a fishtail at dusk, making her the fastest, prettiest creature in the sea. But beware! She'll seduce you into the water, and once you immerse yourself, she'll pull you to the bottom and keep you there. I suggest you avoid prolonged eye contact, so look quickly and move on. Let everyone take a gander at this rare creature."

Flynn heard a splash, so he pushed himself through the spectators and wiggled his way to the rim of an above-ground swimming pool. From this position, he saw a pile of boulders in the center of the pool and water surrounding Cordelia like a moat. She sat on top of the rocks, her fishtail swaying back and forth in the water. Her long, curly, red hair cascaded over her shoulders, and her skin had a hint of freckles. She appeared to be a few years older than Flynn. He marveled at her full, rosy-red lips, and for the life of him, he couldn't figure out how they had made her mermaid tail look so real.

Cordelia's bright-green eyes made contact with Flynn's. She smiled and beckoned him to join her in the pool. He froze at the sight of her beauty and responded with a meek smile.

"You better move on, kid," Salvatore warned as his eyes narrowed and cut Flynn down to size. "She likes you. And that can be dangerous."

A few people chuckled. Embarrassed, Flynn stepped away from the pool, and another person immediately took his place. As he rushed out of the tent, he almost crashed into a muscular man riding a unicycle. Flynn paused for a moment and let the man juggling fire batons ride by.

Flynn walked past the vendors, glancing over their merchandise. He checked his pocket change and realized that most of the items were out of his price range. Another billboard caught his eye: "Expand Your Horizons! Enhance Your Life! Talk with Albert the Fortune Teller!"

Intrigued by the future, Flynn paid the admission fee and entered the tent with great reservation. With the help of a flickering candle on a table, his eyes slowly adjusted to his new surroundings. The Technicolor tent dazzled his eyes; it was decorated with a full spectrum of colors. It had green and red striped walls, and the ceiling had been painted to look like the sky.

What does a fortune-teller know about my future? he wondered as his eyes noticed a sparkling crystal ball resting on the table.

A grumbled voice spoke from behind a star-covered curtain on the back wall: "Please, have a seat."

The voice startled Flynn, but he dutifully sat down. A wrinkled hand slid the curtain open to reveal Albert. He was an old man with untamed hair, a gray mustache, and a face full of wrinkles. His hooded robe draped from his shoulders to his toes. He sat down in an empty chair and squinted at Flynn.

Flynn felt uncomfortable, so he gripped the armrests. His knuckles turned white as the old man silently peered into his eyes. *He's looking straight into my mind,* Flynn feared.

"Relax, young man. The future is going to happen whether you like it or not," Albert finally said. "If you think insecurely, you'll act timid. If you think confidently, you'll act self-assured. If you want to do something bold in life, never let fear overpower you."

Flynn took his advice and released his death grip on the chair. He pretended to be relaxed and placed his hands on the table, palms down. He forced a stern look, but none of this drove his anxiety from his mind.

"So, what would you like to know about your future?" Albert asked with an aura of mystery.

"What should I study in college, and will I ever find a girlfriend?" Flynn blurted out without pause. These questions tortured him, and since he couldn't talk to his parents, maybe a fortune-teller could give him some advice.

Albert leaned forward in his chair and placed bifocals on the bridge of his nose. He scratched his chin with his left hand and slowly waved his right hand over the crystal ball. The candle flame flickered as a breeze passed through the tent, giving Flynn goose bumps. The core of the ball glowed bright amber and purple smoke swirled inside. An expanding universe seemed to be trapped inside the crystal ball.

Transfixed, Albert rambled, "I see that you met a girl at a dance... But you fear that she's out of your league, which makes you extremely shy around her. In fact, you barely talk to her, right?" Flynn's open mouth was all Albert needed to see, so he continued. "You're afraid of rejection, from this girl, from your parents, and from life in general. You're uncomfortable with risks, even though you know what you want. So you sit back instead of taking action because criticism terrifies you."

Surprised by the honesty of Albert's statements, Flynn didn't know how to respond, so he changed the subject and asked, "What about college?"

"Like I said before, you know what you're passionate about, but you're afraid to go after it," Albert responded, drawing from a life full of experiences. "The same obstacles you face in your mind will be lived out in your reality."

Flynn pondered the advice, crossed his arms, and thought, *Is Albert a crazy old man, or does he really understand me?*

Albert raised his eyebrows and asked, "Is there anything else you want to know?"

"No," Flynn said, hesitating slightly, unsure if he had found the answers he was looking for. "I don't have anymore questions."

"Oh, OK," Albert said, looking up from the crystal ball. His shoulders fell as he sat back in his seat, clearly disappointed that Flynn didn't have more questions for him.

Overwhelmed by Albert's insights, Flynn felt light-headed and confused. He had just digested a ton of information and needed fresh air.

Flynn stood up and said, "Thanks for your time."

"Before you go, let me tell you a story about my experience with girls." Albert began reminiscing.

He removed his bifocals and folded his hands as Flynn sat back down.

"Let me tell you kid, fifty years back I was the cat's meow," Albert boasted.

Albert's tone changed then, and he spoke as if he were a teenager, complete with outdated slang.

"I had a gig near Chicago at a speakeasy called the Roarin Twenties, and oh, did I have the moves….in my mind, at least," Albert said without bragging. "I tried to be a cool cat, but I wasn't the smoothest ladies man."

Flynn chuckled at Albert's choice of words and sat up straight in his chair. The way Albert was talking reminded him of his own grandfather.

"I had one thing going for me though, I played a mean piano." Albert continued to stroll down memory lane. "I could tickle the ivories better than anyone around. Well, one night, we had a talent competition, and this beautiful dame named Elsa took the mic and sang 'Flaming Mamie.' She had a voice like butter. Oh, I took one look and cupid's arrow shot through my heart. I was a goner. I couldn't talk around her without getting all flustered." Albert looked animated and alive.

Flynn smiled and nodded; he could relate to the old man's story. He felt the same way about Rena.

"I finally mustered the courage by the end of the night, and asked her to dance." Albert beamed. "I figured it was my only shot and I couldn't let her get away…The rest was history."

"What do you mean?" Flynn leaned forward and raised his eyebrows. "What happened?"

"We got married and Elsa was the love of my life." Albert glowed with pride.

"Where is she now?" Flynn asked with anticipation.

"Unfortunately, she passed away a few years ago," Albert said, his glowing eyes dimmed. "I was blessed with forty seven years before she left this earth, and I'm grateful for every minute."

Flynn's shoulders slumped at the end of Albert's story.

Albert kissed his fingertips, placed them to his heart, and then raised his fingers to the sky as if reaching for his wife. "Love you, honey."

Flynn gave him a small smile.

"So you went for it," Flynn confirmed the moral of the story.

"That's right." Albert nodded with satisfaction. "I took a risk, and I didn't let her walk away."

Flynn stood up and shook Albert's hand. "Thanks for everything."

"Good luck!" Albert said.

Flynn left the tent and paused for a moment as Albert's words echoed through his mind. Out of the corner of his eye, he saw Rena and her family walk into the main circus tent with Salvatore.

6

Tuesday morning...

lynn awoke to the warm glow of a kerosene lantern resting on top of a crate. To his left, he heard the chatter of Sammy and Buster playing cards at a table. To his right, he saw two sleeping bags. Feeling sorry for the clowns' misfortune, Flynn thought, *Salvatore makes them sleep in the back of a truck instead of a camper.*

Sammy and Buster were wearing their clothes from the circus performance but no clown make-up. They had squinty eyes and clean-shaven chins; they looked like brothers. The semitruck hit a bump in the road, and Buster grabbed his soda can before it spilled.

Sammy laid down his cards and said with excitement, "Full house!"

Buster rubbed the back of his neck and pulled a card out of his collar. He dropped his cards on the table and exclaimed, "Sorry, brother, four of a kind!"

"What?" Sammy slammed his fist on the table. "You cheated!"

"No, you dealt me those cards!" Buster countered. He pulled in the cash on the table and asked, "One more game?"

"Fine, one more," Sammy muttered with displeasure.

"I promise, I won't take all your money," Buster mumbled with an unsympathetic smile.

Flynn managed to sit up inside the cage. He yelped in pain when a rabbit mistook his finger for a carrot and nibbled on it.

Sammy and Buster turned around and looked at the rusty cage.

"He's awake," Sammy remarked. "Hey kid, what's your name?"

Flynn remained silent, unsure if he could trust these guys.

Sammy ignored Flynn's silence and waved. "I'm Sammy." Then he pointed across the table. "That's my brother, Buster."

Flynn looked at them quietly.

Buster leaned back in his chair, propped his feet on the table, and asked, "Are you wishing you never came to this circus?"

"Yes," Flynn replied quietly.

"Don't worry. We're not going to hurt you," Sammy reassured him. "We wish we never met Salvatore too."

The truck came to a sudden stop, and the back door flipped open. The sun peeked above the horizon, and a shadowy figure climbed into the truck.

"What's up, Marcel?" Buster asked.

Flynn didn't recognize Marcel. He had shrunk down to a normal-sized person, and his muscles were proportional to that of a body builder.

"We're in another town," Marcel informed them. "Before we set up the circus, Salvatore wants you guys to make breakfast for everyone."

Marcel turned around and opened up the rabbit cage. He grabbed Flynn by the arm and pulled him out.

"Kid, help them with breakfast," Marcel snipped.

Flynn stretched his limbs and tried to get the blood flowing through his legs. He thought about running, but he didn't know if anyone would stop him. He decided to play it safe and wait for an opportunity to escape when no one was looking. He quietly helped the brothers unload boxes and coolers from the semitruck. He set up card tables and two camper stoves. Sammy turned on the stoves while Flynn and Buster unloaded eggs, bacon, and hashbrowns from a cooler.

Sammy pointed to a box. "Why don't you set the tables?"

Flynn grabbed some plates, utensils, and napkins out of the box. His stomach grumbled from a mixture of hunger and nerves.

Buster fried the bacon while Sammy cooked the eggs. Sammy needed a spatula, so he stretched his arm and grabbed two utensils out of a box several feet away without leaving the stove. Flynn looked astonished at Sammy's elastic arm.

Sammy laughed and asked, "Pretty cool, huh?"

"Yeah!" Flynn nodded. "How did you do that?"

"Well," Sammy explained, "Buster and I were looking for work as rodeo clowns. We couldn't find any work, so we answered an ad in the paper for circus clowns instead. When we met Salvatore, he said he could turn us into the best rodeo clowns in the world. At first, we didn't believe him, but then he introduced us to Jack and Marcel. When we saw their talents, we signed up."

"Salvatore gives people supernatural powers?" Flynn asked, a flood of questions now running through his mind.

"No, but Albert can," Buster said.

"The fortune-teller?" Flynn asked, surprised.

"Yeah, Albert can turn any talent into a super talent," Buster explained.

Flynn was puzzled, so Buster continued. "Marcel won tons of body builder competitions, so Albert gave him superhuman strength. Jack was a zookeeper, but now he can change any animal into another animal. I don't know how, but Salvatore can manipulate time."

Stunned by all the information, Flynn thought, *How can I escape? Salvatore is too powerful.*

"My name is Flynn." He began to trust them a little.

"Nice to meet you," Sammy said genuinely.

Sammy grabbed two empty plates and loaded them with omelets covered with cheese.

He handed them to Flynn and said, "Take these to Salvatore." Sammy pointed to an expensive black motor home. "He's in that one."

"Not me," Flynn replied reluctantly.

"Better you than me." Sammy chuckled and pushed him toward the motor home.

Flynn cautiously carried the plates to the RV and knocked on the door with his elbow. When Salvatore opened the door, he was holding a brown paper bag.

"About time. I'm starving," Salvatore growled.

Inside the dimly lit RV, Flynn saw a few physics books on a coffee table, two leather recliner chairs, and a porcelain flower pot in between the chairs. To his left, he noticed a kitchen and dining room squeezed inside the motor home. Flynn was startled when he saw Cordelia sitting at the table. She had legs and feet, but no fishtail. She briefly smiled at Flynn. Salvatore ignored them while he emptied the paper bag's content onto the table. Flynn's eyes popped as wads of cash and jewelry were spread out onto the table. Cordelia picked up Deana's bracelet and placed it around her wrist. Her eyes lit up as she looked over the rest of the jewelry.

"Thanks, Dad!" Cordelia exclaimed.

Salvatore sat down, counted the money on the table, and said, "You're welcome, sweetheart. I have some clothes too." He pointed to Deana's designer clothes in a nearby suitcase.

At that moment, Flynn realized why Salvatore had wanted Deana's clothes; she was roughly the same size as Cordelia.

Without looking up, Salvatore barked, "Kid, leave the plates on the table."

BANG! The motor home door had slammed shut.

Startled by the loud noise, Flynn almost dropped the plates on the floor. He quickly recovered and placed the plates on the table before the food spilled.

"Marcel, is that you?" Salvatore called-out.

In a low, gruff voice, an old man replied, "No, it's your father."

Flynn turned around and saw Albert the fortune-teller.

"Dad, you're awake?" Salvatore asked, surprised by his father's presence.

"Yes, I'm awake." Albert walked into the room with the help of a cane and tapped Flynn's shoulder and asked, "Who's this?"

"I hired a new employee," Salvatore stated calmly. "His name is Flynn Parkes."

Albert looked into Flynn's eyes and remarked, "Aren't you kind of young to join the circus?"

"He's old enough," Salvatore responded before Flynn could say a word.

Albert saw the pile of cash and asked, "Did you perform a private show for another wealthy family?"

"Yes, I did," Salvatore said without a look of guilt or regret.

"Did they pay willingly?" Albert asked skeptically.

Salvatore paused for a moment before answering, "Yes."

"Don't lie to me!" Albert said with a scowl.

Flynn didn't want to get involved in the argument, so he kept his mouth shut. Cordelia squirmed in her chair, clearly upset. She looked guilty, as if she had betrayed her grandfather.

Salvatore justified his position by saying, "I'm trying to run a profitable business."

"Our job is to entertain people, not steal from them!" Albert asserted.

"We don't make money when I do it your way!" Salvatore raised his voice.

Cordelia became teary-eyed as her father and grandfather continued to argue. Flynn felt uncomfortable.

"Remember, I'm still in charge." Albert stood his ground. "I'm not dead, and until then, you don't own this circus!"

Salvatore's face turned red, and he glared at Flynn. "What are you looking at? Get out!"

Flynn panicked and ran out the camper door. He heard more shouting as he scurried to the picnic tables. Relieved to get out of that situation, he jumped behind Marcel in the food line. Marcel filled his plate and took a seat next to Jack. Not sure where to go, Flynn grabbed some food and sat across from them.

"Sounds like they're fighting again," Marcel said with frustration. "I didn't sign up for this mess."

"I don't know why Albert is upset. We're making tons of money." Jack looked confused. "And you? What are you complaining about?"

"You paid off your debt to Salvatore, and now you're sharing in the profits," Marcel said. "I'm still working off my contract. I don't like being his servant and ripping people off."

"You're the strongest person on earth," Jack pointed out. "After another year, you can do whatever you want."

"Yeah, if Salvatore lets me," Marcel retorted.

"Free will, Marcel, free will," Jack stated bluntly.

Flynn heard the camper door slam and they looked over to see Albert hobbling along with his cane. Cordelia ran after him, wiping away her tears. Albert shook his head and mumbled something under his breath. She consoled him by rubbing his shoulder.

"Staring again?" Jack taunted.

"What?" Flynn asked. Jack's comment baffled him.

"Not you," Jack said. "Him." He pointed to Marcel.

Marcel was transfixed on Cordelia. His eyes glazed over as if lost in his own little world.

Jack gave Marcel a nudge.

Marcel awakened from his daydream. "Huh? What'd you say?"

"Are you fantasizing about Cordelia again?" Jack teased.

"No!" Marcel shook his head. "Shut up!"

"Forget about her," Jack advised. "Salvatore would never let her date the help."

Marcel's shoulders slumped, and he looked defeated.

Salvatore stormed out of the camper and marched over to the picnic tables.

"Listen up!" Salvatore said, all revved up. "We have a lot to do before tonight's show. Jack, make Flynn clean out the animal cages. Sammy and Buster, you can help Flynn after you wash the dishes. Bring the kid back to me when you're done. Everyone else, let's get the tents set up!"

"Come on kid. Follow me," Jack snipped.

The campground had a hose spigot, which Jack used to fill a bucket with soap and water. He grabbed a sponge and cleaning supplies out of the truck and handed them to Flynn. The rabbit cage sat on the ground next to the semitruck. Jack opened the cage door and placed the rabbits on the ground. He petted them, and they quickly transformed into two lions and a lioness.

"Don't even think about trying to escape," Jack warned. "The lions are fast, and they haven't had their breakfast." He pointed to a bale of hay and said, "When you're done cleaning, put fresh hay on the floor. After that, Sammy and Buster can show you how to clean the rhino cages."

Jack walked away as the lions licked their lips and laid down. The lioness looked at Flynn with an intense stare and clawed the ground. *Why did Jack leave me alone with the lions? What if they attack me?* Flynn worried.

Flynn pulled the dirty hay from the cage and threw it into a garbage can. He grabbed the sponge, dipped it into the bucket, and scrubbed the metal bars. He started to sweat in the early morning sun. He wiped his brow and placed the sponge back into the bucket.

The lioness dominated the situation. She yawned and sprawled on the ground, lazily watching Flynn put clean hay into the cage. When he was finished, he looked down and noticed the lions had closed their eyes and had fallen asleep. Flynn looked around and saw no one in sight. When they didn't stir, he tiptoed past the lions and broke into a run.

The lions awakened from their slumber when they heard the crunching sound of Flynn's sneakers treading on the gravel several yards away. They sprang to their feet as Flynn ran into a forest on the outskirts of the campground. There was no path to follow, so Flynn stomped through the dense bushes. Several yards in, he came to a steep hill. Without slowing down, he clawed his way upward. He heard the lions' grunts and pants getting closer. Glancing over his shoulder, he saw the lions closing in on him, their jaws open and saliva dripping off their chins. Distracted by his fear, Flynn didn't notice the tree root in front of him; he tripped and fell face first onto the ground. He rushed to regain his footing, but gravity took over. He tumbled down the hill a few feet until his body slammed against a tree. Wincing in pain, he stood up. The lions circled around him. Frantically, he saw a low-hanging branch, so he climbed up the tree. The lions growled and pawed at the bark as the lioness climbed after Flynn.

"Help me!" Flynn yelled, his voice echoing through the forest.

He glanced down at the lioness that was now inches from his feet. Feeling trapped, he gasped and shimmied out onto a tree limb. The lioness shook the limb with her paw, forcing Flynn to wrap his arms and legs tighter around the branch. He heard the crackling sound of the branch giving way beneath him, and they tumbled to the ground. The lions quickly surrounded him, leaving no room for escape. Flynn covered his head with his hands, violent images filling his thoughts.

7

~

Sammy and Buster must have heard Flynn's scream for help. They ran
through the forest and waved their arms, trying to distract the lions
from their prey. The lions turned around and growled at the clowns.

"Jack!" Sammy shouted. "Call off your lions!"

Jack emerged from behind some trees and said, "What are you guys
afraid of? They're harmless."

How can Jack be so calm? Flynn thought. *Does he even have a conscience?*

"Yeah, right." Buster looked furious. "Whatever you say!"

Without a shred of fear, Jack strolled over to the lions and petted
them. One by one they transformed back into harmless rabbits.

"Kid," Jack asked with amusement, "did you pee your pants?"

Flynn didn't laugh at the joke.

Sammy and Buster helped Flynn off the ground.

"I told you they would chase after you," Jack said with a scowl. "I
warned you. You don't listen, do you?"

Flynn didn't respond, and instead, he brushed the dirt off his pants;
his knees were still shaking.

Jack picked up the rabbits, handed them to Flynn, and commanded,
"You carry them."

The rabbits squirmed harmlessly in Flynn's arms as they walked
back to the campground.

"Let's keep this a secret," Jack said looking at Sammy. "I don't want
Salvatore blowing a gasket 'cuz we didn't watch the kid close enough."

"Fine, but you owe us one," Sammy said angrily. "Technically, you're the one who let the kid out of *your* sight."

"OK, OK," Jack grumbled.

∽◯

Flynn placed the rabbits onto the new bed of hay and closed the cage door.

As Jack walked away, he jabbed, "Have fun cleaning out the rhino cage. Ha-ha."

"Thanks!" Sammy replied unenthusiastically.

Buster pinched his nose, then looked at Flynn and said, "Rhino cages get pretty smelly."

Flynn followed them to the back of another semitruck. Sammy and Buster pulled on two straps and a ramp rolled along metal tracks underneath the bed of the truck. They dropped the end of the ramp on the ground. The brothers then opened the door, revealing the rhino.

"Flynn, could you grab a hose in the cab and hook it up to the water spigot?" Sammy requested as he guided the animal down the ramp by its reins.

Flynn nodded and ran to the cab of the truck. He looked everywhere.

"I can't find it!" Flynn yelled out the truck window.

"Look behind the seat!" Buster yelled back.

Flynn found the hose hidden underneath a blanket. He ran the hose over to the faucet, attached it to the spigot, and brought the other end to Buster. Sammy stuck a spike into the ground and tied the rhino to it. Flynn turned on the faucet while Buster sprayed the floor of the truck trailer.

As they cleaned, Buster joked, "Why do we get all the crappy jobs?"

"'Cuz we're at the beginning of our contracts. Soon, we'll be making big money!" Sammy reminded Buster. "And the new guys will get to clean the cages."

"What's the contract everyone talks about?" Flynn asked. He didn't know anything about a "contract." He trusted Sammy and Buster would give him truthful answers. All things considered, they did save him from the lions.

"Everyone signed a contract with Salvatore," Sammy explained. "It says if we receive a special talent, we *have* to work for him for two years. After that, we can share in the profits from the circus."

"Why?" Flynn asked, trying to understand their motives.

"We wanted to be great entertainers," Buster said with regret. "But we didn't realize the price we would have to pay."

"How long do you have left?" Flynn asked; he could relate to their misfortune.

"One year and six months," Sammy replied sadly.

"And two hours and fifty minutes," Buster added. "But who's counting?"

"Does Albert know about the contract?" Flynn asked.

"No," Buster said sternly. "Salvatore said if we told Albert, he would erase our memories."

"Wow, erase your memories!" The idea astounded Flynn. "Then who's in charge?"

"I thought Albert was in charge, but I don't know anymore." Sammy looked worried.

"I heard that when Albert dies, Salvatore will inherit the circus," Buster said with disgust.

"I hope not," Sammy said somberly. "I don't want to work for him forever."

"Me either," Buster agreed. "The only reason I stick around is because I don't want to lose my memory."

"What about the other employees?" Flynn probed. "Did they sign a contract too?"

"Not yet," Sammy shook his head.

"Why do they stay?" Flynn asked.

"Because they want special talents," Buster explained. "They want what we have. If they serve loyally, Salvatore will let them become circus performers and share in the wealth. Fear and greed keep them trapped."

It felt like an oven in the back of the truck. Buster sprayed the floor with a hose while Sammy and Flynn scrubbed it with mops. Other than chores at home, Flynn had never done any real work, not even a summer job. Flynn didn't breathe through his nose; the smell of excrement overwhelmed him. After cleaning up the mess, Sammy led the rhinoceros back inside the truck and locked the door.

"You can take the kid to Salvatore." Buster pushed off his responsibility.

"No, that's all right, you can do it." Sammy smiled. "Salvatore's *your* buddy."

"Thanks, brother," Buster scoffed.

"You're welcome." Sammy laughed.

Buster dropped his shoulders, looked at Flynn and said reluctantly, "Come on. Follow me."

As Flynn sulked behind Buster, he asked, "Why don't you want to talk to Salvatore?"

"He treats everyone like dirt," Buster said plainly. Before walking into the main tent Buster added, "Salvatore is all about money; Albert is all about people."

Inside the tent, Flynn saw the trapeze equipment set up in the center ring. Rego hung by his knees on a trapeze bar and swung back and forth. Paula jumped off a platform, grabbed a trapeze bar, and used her weight as momentum to sync with Rego's swing. She backflipped off the trapeze bar and Rego caught her. In unison, they both swung back to the platform.

Without warning, Paula took a swan dive off the platform. As she fell, she arched her back, spread out her arms, and sprouted white wings. She swooped upward in an arc, barely hitting the ground.

Salvatore, who sat in the bleachers, applauded. He strolled over to Flynn and said, "We're going to practice a new routine. We're going to shoot you from a cannon, and Rego is going to catch you."

Flynn's stomach twisted up inside when he looked up at Rego on the high platform.

"What about a net?" Flynn asked nervously.

"We don't use nets around here." Salvatore smirked.

"I-I-I ca-ca-can't do that!" Flynn stuttered.

Flynn spun around and ran for the exit. Salvatore pulled out his pocket watch and swung it back and forth, freezing Flynn in his tracks. Buster grabbed Flynn under his arms and dragged him back. Salvatore stopped the watch and Flynn unfroze.

"You can't run away. You owe me!" Salvatore reminded Flynn. Salvatore pointed to a cannon set up in the back of the tent and said, "Get to work!"

Flynn shrunk back into his insecurity. With no options, he reluctantly ran over to the cannon and climbed into the barrel.

When can I make my own decisions without being told what to do? Flynn wondered, frustrated with his life.

Buster stood behind the cannon and shouted, "Five, four, three, two, one!" Buster lit the fuse.

KA-BOOM!

Flynn's body shot high into the air. Oxygen was sucked out of his lungs, and his head barely skimmed the ceiling. He extended his hands, hoping Rego would catch him, but he was moving too fast. He felt Rego's hand brush past his arms. Flynn lost momentum and fell toward the ground. He covered his eyes with his arms and braced for impact.

Paula flew in and caught him a split second before he hit the ground. Flynn's heart beat rapidly, and his knees almost collapsed when she set him down next to Salvatore.

"Thanks…for…catching me!" Flynn exclaimed breathlessly.

"No problem, kid," Paula said in a comforting voice.

"I guess that needs work." Salvatore shook his head and laughed. "Geez, are you good at anything, kid?"

Deflated by the question, Flynn shrugged his shoulders. It seemed he didn't have any skills.

"Make yourself useful and go find something you *can* do," Salvatore said flatly. "Buster, follow him so he doesn't run away."

"OK, boss," Buster replied obediently and led Flynn outside.

Flynn saw Albert a few yards away sitting on a stool next to a pile of canvas and tent poles. He appeared to be exhausted and frustrated.

"Are you OK?" Buster asked as they approached Albert.

"I'm getting too old for this." Albert panted. "I need help setting up the tent."

Without saying a word, Flynn grabbed a tent stake and hammer and drove he stake into the ground. Buster pitched in and helped Flynn set up the fortune-tellers' tent.

"Thanks a million guys," Albert said with gratitude as they all worked under the afternoon sun.

"No problem. Anytime," Flynn replied. He was glad to help the kind old man.

Albert studied Flynn's face. "I recognize you. You stopped by my tent last night."

"Yeah, I did," Flynn replied.

"You were asking about girls," Albert recalled. "They're a mystery, I give you that, but you have trouble with girls because you're shy."

Flynn blushed. He knew that; he just didn't know how to fix it.

"I have an idea." Albert smiled.

He disappeared for a few minutes and returned with Cordelia.

Flynn's stomach felt like it had butterflies, and his forehead began to sweat. In addition to his usual insecurities around girls, Flynn knew he probably looked and smelled terrible.

Albert made the introduction. "Flynn, I want you to meet my grand-daughter Cordelia."

"Hi, Flynn." Cordelia gave Flynn a coy smile. Looking at her grand-father, she added, "We met at breakfast."

Not sure of what to say, Flynn gave her a small wave and went back to setting up the tent.

"Oh, come on. You can do better than that!" Albert encouraged, try-ing to coach Flynn along. "Put down the hammer and come over here."

Flynn put down the hammer and took a few steps toward her.

"Good," Albert complimented him. "Now stand up straight, look her in the eye, and greet her properly."

Flynn squared his shoulders, extended his hand, and looked into Cordelia's bewitching green eyes.

"Now, repeat after me," Albert said. "'Cordelia, it's nice to meet you.'"

Flynn gently shook her hand and quietly repeated the words. "Hi, um, Cordelia, it's, um, very nice to meet you."

"You're getting there, but I know you can do even better." Albert didn't let Flynn off the hook just yet. "Now ask her a question, but this time, try speaking a little louder and clearer."

Flynn mustered some courage, cleared his throat and reminded himself to maintain eye contact with Cordelia. "How are you today?" he asked.

"Good." She giggled nervously as she shot her grandpa the evil eye. "How long are you going to be with us?"

After a long moment of silence, Albert nudged Flynn. "Don't be shy; answer her."

Flynn's body flinched a bit before he blurted out, "I don't know. I just started working here today."

"Well, I hope you stick around for awhile," she said with a friendly smile.

He couldn't answer her honestly, so he smiled politely. He had no idea who he could trust at the circus. All he wanted to do was go home.

Albert chuckled and whispered in Flynn's ear, "She's single, young man."

Flynn blushed.

"You have a cool circus," Flynn said to Cordelia, realizing how corny it sounded the minute the words escaped his lips. He wanted to crawl under a rock and hide, but she bailed him out.

"Thanks!" Cordelia replied. "You want to see something really cool?"

"Sure," Flynn said with mixed emotions. Every second spent with her opened himself up to more risk. He worried he might do something embarrassing or get into trouble.

"Buster, do you need anymore help?" Flynn asked, throwing a little caution to the wind.

"No, I'm good," Buster said while setting up the last tent pole. Keeping Flynn on a tight leash, he added, "I'll catch up with you in a minute."

"OK," Flynn replied.

"Follow me," Cordelia said.

Flynn noticed that she walked with a slight limp instead of taking long strides. Fearing rejection, he said nothing. *What does she want to show me?* he wondered, feeling nervous and excited at the same time.

8

~

ordelia led Flynn to her pearl-white camper, opened the door, and they stepped inside. His eyes popped when he saw a huge fish aquarium. It was taller than Flynn and about eighteen feet long. He'd never seen an aquarium that size. Clown fish, lionfish, and several blue lace fish swam inside the tank. At the bottom were polished rocks, shells, chunks of coral, and Petoskey stones. Several green lamps lit the back of the tank.

"Wow! That's awesome!" he exclaimed as he gazed at the fish swimming back and forth between clumps of seaweed. For a brief moment, the stress of his situation melted away.

"Sometimes I come here when I want to feel alive," Cordelia explained. "Especially, when I'm far away from any water."

A loud knock on the camper door interrupted the moment. Worried it might be Salvatore, Flynn stood behind Cordelia as she opened the door.

He saw Marcel holding onto his bike.

"Hey, that's mine!" Flynn exclaimed. He'd forgotten all about it.

"Not anymore," Marcel sneered in jest. "Finders, keepers."

"Marcel, don't be a jerk," Cordelia said.

"OK, Cordelia." Marcel backed down. He obviously didn't want to get on her bad side. "I was just kidding. Kid, you can have it back." Marcel pretended to be friendly, but he couldn't keep up the act. "What are you doing in Cordelia's camper?"

"Nothing." Flynn gulped, feeling guilty for no reason.

"I was showing him my aquarium," Cordelia fired back. "But that's none of your business." Marcel didn't seem to frighten her.

Marcel shrunk a little and responded, "Your dad opened the gates to the public. I'm supposed to keep Flynn busy while everyone entertains the crowd."

"OK," Cordelia said sternly. "Go easy on him."

Flynn's heart filled with gloom while his stomach twisted up inside. He preferred to stay with Cordelia. She was more fun and exciting to be around.

Marcel scowled at Flynn and said, "Follow me."

Flynn and Marcel put the bike inside the semitruck with the rabbit cage. As he tried to keep up, Flynn sprinted behind Marcel in silence. They entered the main tent through the back entrance. In the back of tent was a small dressing room. A few dressers and chairs sat next to a makeup counter and mirror. A unicycle leaned against a wooden stool. The seat sat on the ground while the wheel spun in the air.

Marcel grabbed duct tape from the dresser drawer and growled, "Put your hands together."

"Why?" Flynn asked in a shaky voice.

"Just do it." Marcel snapped.

The hair on the back of Flynn's neck stood up, and a chill tingled down his spine. Flynn placed his shaky hands together while Marcel wrapped duct tape around his wrists.

Marcel then pushed down on Flynn's shoulders and commanded him to take a seat.

Flynn tried to resist, but Marcel's arms were too strong, and Flynn sank into a chair in front of the make-up counter.

Marcel grabbed some rope and said, "Sorry, kid. Salvatore wants to keep you quiet for a few hours."

He wrapped the rope around Flynn's waist and arms. He tied knots behind the back of the chair so Flynn couldn't stand up. The rope squeezed Flynn's arms like a python snake and dug into his skin. He felt the veins in his hands being choked from the lack of blood flowing through his body.

"When you were in Cordelia's trailer, did she say anything about me?"

Flynn squirmed in his seat and replied, "No."

Marcel placed duct tape over Flynn's mouth and proclaimed angrily, "Wrong answer. If you can change that, then maybe I'll help you."

Flynn's glimmer of hope vanished when Marcel grunted and disappeared into the evening. Pushing away feelings of despair, Flynn looked around the room for a knife to cut himself loose. He saw a few open drawers, so he jostled his chair over to them. Leaning back, he looked inside the dresser. He couldn't find a knife or any sharp objects. He tried to slither out of the ropes, but the knot tightened even more. When he heard loud voices outside the tent, he yelled for help, but the duct tape muffled the sound of his voice.

Desperation crept into his thoughts. He wished he could go back in time and make different decisions. He missed his parents and the security of his home. He wondered if he would survive or if the police would find him.

After what seemed like several hours, the voices of the crowd subsided, signaling closing time.

Marcel reentered the dressing room and declared with excitement, "It's show time!"

Over the speakers, Flynn heard Salvatore announce, "Welcome to the greatest show on earth. Prepare to be entertained by Sammy and Buster the clowns!"

Marcel opened a dresser drawer, took out a pair of gym shorts, and put them on.

"My clothes are as delicate as lace, but as strong as iron," Marcel bragged. "Salvatore invented the fabric so it could stretch to fit my body, and Cordelia sewed it together for me."

Marcel grabbed some heavy dumbbells that were sitting next to the dresser and curled them. The more energy he used to work out, the more his muscles bulged and his body grew taller. Slowly, his body expanded into that of a gigantic weight lifter, standing nearly twenty feet tall. After completing his transformation, he peered around the curtain separating the dressing room from the circus.

Flynn heard Salvatore shout, "Prepare to be amazed by the power of Marcel the Champ!"

That was Marcel's cue, and he walked to the center ring.

Jack strolled into the dressing room, glanced at Flynn, and laughed. He didn't appear shocked or even concerned about Flynn's predicament.

"In trouble again?" Jack asked. "You can't run away. Salvatore will never let that happen. By the way, a detective was here earlier asking questions. I think his name was Winslow, I can't remember. Anyway, he had a photo of you, but don't get your hopes up. Salvatore said he saw you leave with some kids the other night." Jack chuckled. "Salvatore was very convincing, even when he hypnotized the detective with his pocket watch."

Flynn was devastated by the news. *A detective came to ask questions and Salvatore lied to him! Now what am I going to do?* he asked himself.

"I would like to stay and chat, but I need to find some rascally rabbits," Jack joked as he exited the back of the tent.

After a few minutes, Jack returned with three rabbits. He stood by the curtain and waited for Salvatore's cue.

"Hmm." Jack peaked out from the curtain and got excited. "Looks like a *really* rich family. We're going to have an extra-large payday!"

Flynn heard Salvatore shout, "For the next act, we'll need a volunteer."

Jack set the rabbits on the ground and grabbed two Hula-Hoops that had been leaning against the dresser. The rabbits hopped behind Jack as he walked out to the center ring.

After he left, Albert crept into the dressing room. His eyes widened when he saw Flynn tied to a chair.

"What the heck is going on?" Albert exclaimed.

Flynn yelped in pain when Albert ripped the duct tape off his mouth.

"Who did this to you?" Albert asked, cutting Flynn loose with a pocketknife.

Flynn's arms tingled as blood began flowing through his body again. He shook his arms so could regain movement in his limbs.

"Marcel," Flynn answered, rubbing his sore wrists.

"Why would Marcel tie you up?" Albert asked.

"Salvatore told him to. He doesn't want me to run away. Salvatore kidnapped me." Flynn sighed in exasperation.

"What?" Albert asked.

Flynn tried to stand up, but his legs had fallen asleep and still felt numb.

"I need to talk to Salvatore," Albert said with distress. "Where is he?"

Flynn massaged his legs and replied, "He's out there putting on a show."

Flynn struggled to follow Albert through the curtain.

They saw Salvatore standing in front of the bleachers. Inside the center ring, a young boy holding two Hula-Hoops stood in front of Jack. Jack bent down and petted the two rabbits. As they passed through the center of the hoops, the rabbits morphed into full-size lions. They landed on the ground and turned menacingly toward the boy.

"Stop the show!" Albert yelled, glaring at Salvatore "Are you a madman?"

"I'm not a madman. I'm just a man!" Salvatore sneered with wild eyes.

The boy's parents leaped from the bleachers and ran toward to the stage to rescue their child.

Salvatore held up his pocket watch and froze the lions and the boy in place. He raised his hand and proclaimed, "I've got this under control. Marcel, make his parents sit down!"

Marcel blocked the parents from running to their son.

"What are you doing?" Albert yelled.

"Making money!" Salvatore shouted back.

"For the last time, we use our talents to help people, not steal from them!" Albert exclaimed. "This is your last chance. Stop this behavior or lose your powers."

"I'm in charge now!" Salvatore responded angrily.

"You leave me no choice," Albert proclaimed. "I'm taking away your powers."

"No. You won't!" Salvatore protested.

Albert raised his hands and chanted, "I call on the four classical elements, wind, fire, earth, and water. Wind moves sand. Fire creates…"

Before he could finish his chant, Jack bent down and petted the third rabbit. The rabbit lunged through the air, transformed into a lioness, and pounced on Albert, pinning him to the ground. Flynn stood motionless, watching in total shock as the scene unfolded.

The lioness growled and almost mauled Albert when Salvatore raised his pocket watch. Albert and the lioness froze in time.

"That should keep them busy for awhile," Salvatore boasted confidently. "Let's see, where was I?" Salvatore turned back to the terrified parents and said, "Ah, yes, back to business. Like I said earlier, the show is priceless. What are you willing to pay for the safety of your child?"

"What do you want?" the mother cried, gripping her husband's arm.

"Bring all of your money and jewelry to me," Salvatore ordered. "If you're not back by midnight, or if you go to the police, this will be your boy's final act."

Without hesitation, the parents rushed out of the tent. Flynn calmed down a bit and regained his senses. He made a run for the dressing room, but Marcel saw him out of the corner of his eye. He swung his pocket watch, stopping Flynn in his tracks. Marcel tucked Flynn under his arm, and brought him to Salvatore. Salvatore stopped swinging his pocket watch and Flynn unfroze.

"How did you do that?" Flynn exclaimed in amazement.

"Space and time are relative to the observer." Salvatore grinned. "There's the arrow of time that happens at the atomic level. There's the psychological timeline that each individual perceives. And there's the timeline of the universe. I slowed your motion through time. People see the world in three dimensions: height, width, and depth. Sometimes, they forget about the fourth dimension, time."

Salvatore patted Flynn on the head and said, "You have a lot to learn." Then he scowled at Marcel and said, "I told you to keep a better eye on Albert and the kid."

"OK boss." Marcel didn't look into Salvatore's eyes, appearing afraid of losing his memory.

Everyone waited inside the tent for the parents to return. Flynn nervously paced the floor, feeling like a trapped animal. Salvatore gave him an angry glance, so he stopped pacing.

After an hour, the parents returned and laid a suitcase full of money and jewelry at Salvatore's feet.

"Sammy, Buster!" Salvatore shouted. "Take it to my camper."

Jack brushed his hand over the two lions, turning them back into rabbits. Salvatore used his pocket watch to unfreeze the circus act. The boy awakened from the trance and ran into his parents' arms.

Hypnotizing the family with the pocket watch, Salvatore said in a soothing voice, "When you wake up, all you'll remember is that you had a great time at the circus. You won't remember or wonder what happened to your money or jewelry."

Salvatore snapped his fingers, and the family rubbed their eyes as if they had awakened from a deep sleep.

The father yawned and exclaimed, "The show was excellent!"

"I'm glad you had a good time." Salvatore said ecstatically. "Tell all of your friends."

After the family left, Jack petted the lioness, turning her back into a rabbit. Salvatore unfroze Albert's timeline and erased his memory of the last two hours.

Still on the ground, Albert asked, "What happened?"

"You fainted," Salvatore replied.

"I remember walking into the tent, but everything after that is blank." Albert looked dazed.

"Marcel found you," Salvatore said, pretending to be puzzled. "He carried you in here so we could keep an eye on you. Are you all right?"

"Yes, I feel fine," Albert reassured everyone.

Salvatore grabbed Albert's arms and helped him off the ground, then said, "Did you take your pills for Alzheimer's and dementia?"

"Yes, I think so," Albert speculated.

"I'll have Marcel check up on you," Salvatore said with false concern. "To make sure you take your pills and you don't have any more lapses of memory."

"I feel lighted-headed. I'm going to bed." Albert rubbed his forehead as he left the main tent.

"OK. Good night, Dad," Salvatore said in a kind voice.

Flynn wanted to yell out the truth and warn Albert, but he knew Salvatore would retaliate.

Salvatore turned to his crew and barked, "Marcel, lock the kid inside the rabbit cage. The rest of you, let's pack up our equipment and head to the next town."

Marcel picked up the rabbits in one hand and he grabbed Flynn by the waist with the other, throwing him over his shoulder. He took them to the cage, stuffed them inside, and locked the cage door with a padlock.

"Stop getting me into trouble and do what you're told!" Marcel snarled. "I don't like getting yelled at."

"OK," Flynn muttered without protest.

"Good," Marcel grumbled.

Marcel shoved them into the semitruck and slammed the door.

Flynn's eyes slowly adjusted to the dark surroundings as he lay down on a clean bed of hay. A million thoughts ran through his mind: his parents, Rena at the school dance, and Cordelia's bewitching green eyes. He drifted in and out of sleep before he heard the truck's engine start. Flynn felt the truck rock back and forth. *Where are we going? What's going to happen next?* he wondered as he fell asleep with his memories.

9

~

Tuesday morning…

Rena, who was a night owl, woke up to the irritating buzz of her alarm clock. Lying in bed, she debated whether or not to get up. She glanced up at her bedroom walls and admired the posters of her favorite bands like The White Stripes and The Black Keys. One poster seemed out of place. It was a print of Vermeer's *Girl, Interrupted at Her Music*. It reminded her to never let anything interrupt her passion for music.

Suddenly, Rena heard loud thumping and crashing sounds from the adjacent bedroom.

"*Oh my gosh! Mom!*" Rena heard Deana's scream.

Rena jumped out of bed to investigate the commotion.

Deana's bedroom door was wide open, and the scene was in total chaos. Dressers were tipped over and drawers were sprawled all across the floor. Dirty footprints were smeared in the carpet. The closet was empty except for bare clothes hangers.

In a state of shock, Mrs. Gainsborough peered over Rena's shoulder and asked, "What happened?"

"I don't know!" Deana said, breathing heavily. "Someone took all my clothes. Maybe we were robbed."

"I didn't hear anything last night," Mrs. Gainsborough said; she checked the bedroom window to see if it was locked.

"I didn't hear anything either," Deana said and shook her head.

"What about you, Rena?" Mrs. Gainsborough asked.

"No," Rena said, not recalling any odd noises.

"I need to tell your dad, but he left for work already," Mrs. Gainsborough said, panic in her voice. "Get dressed and I'll drop you girls off at school, then I'll go talk to your dad."

"Mom!" Deana exclaimed. "How can I go to school? I have nothing to wear!"

"Pick something out in Rena's closet," Mrs. Gainsborough shot back.

"Ewww," Deana said, sticking up her nose. "Her clothes are so... retro."

"Just do it and don't argue with me," Mrs. Gainsborough said in frustration.

"OK," Deana pouted.

～◯

Mrs. Gainsborough quickly dropped her daughters off at school. The two girls scurried to their lockers and gathered their books.

Out of the corner of her eye, Rena noticed Principal Vernon open the door to his office.

"Mr. and Mrs. Parkes, please follow me," Mr. Vernon said.

Parkes? Why are Flynn's parents here? Rena wondered.

Principal Vernon beckoned them with a wave, and they followed him down the hall. Rena noticed that Flynn's dad had an unshaven chin and his clothes were disheveled, like he had left the house in a hurry. Flynn's mom looked agitated and nervous.

What's going on? Rena thought.

They passed Rena and walked over to John, who gathered his books from his locker. Rena overheard their conversation.

"John," Principal Vernon spoke with authority. "We need to ask you a few questions about Flynn."

"Sure." John said in a cooperative voice.

"Have you seen or talked to Flynn?" Mr. Parkes asked sharply.

"The last time I saw him was after school yesterday. He rode his bike past the football field."

"Did he call you or spend the night at your house?" Mrs. Parkes asked earnestly.

"No." John looked perplexed. "Why? What's going on?"

"We haven't seen him since last night," Mr. Parkes said wearily.

"Whoa! What happened?" John asked, concerned.

"We think he ran away." Mr. Parkes speculated.

John's jaw dropped in complete surprise.

"Oh no!" Rena whispered, shocked by the news. Her heart beat a little faster.

"Ray, it's your fault! You're too hard on him. Your non-stop lectures drove him away." Mrs. Parkes scolded him.

"I know." Mr. Parkes consoled his wife by rubbing her shoulder. "I was tough on him, but life is tough and I want him to make smart choices."

"No, Ray, you mean *your* choices!" Mrs. Parkes pushed away her husband's hand as she wiped away her tears.

Mr. Parkes's arms fell to his sides, unsure how to respond to his wife's anger. He turned pale with guilt and regret.

"I'm sure he's OK," Principal Vernon reassured them. "I know teenagers; sometimes they need to blow off some steam."

"I hope you're right," Mrs. Parkes said, a glimmer of hope in her voice.

"I'll talk to Flynn's teachers and see if they have any information," Principal Vernon added. "What's your next move?"

"We're going to the police station to report him missing," Mr. Parkes said. "Then we're going to search for him around town."

"Can I help you look?" John volunteered.

"That would be great," Mr. Parkes said.

"Can I help too?" Rena interrupted.

"Yes! We could use the help," Mrs. Parkes's face lit up. "Are you a friend of Flynn?"

"Well…" Rena hesitated. "Sort of."

Mr. Parkes looked at his wife and whispered, "Flynn never said he had a girlfriend."

"No." Rena blushed and quickly clarified. "Technically, we've never gone out or anything, but we have art and band class together."

"Oh," Mrs. Parkes said, ignoring Rena's awkwardness. "What's your name?"

"Rena. Rena Gainsborough."

"I'm Georgia Parkes, and this is my husband Ray."

"You're Thomas Gainsborough's daughter," Ray said.

"Yes, I am." Rena nodded and shook both their hands.

"John, you have our number. Call us if you find him or hear anything," Georgia requested as she looked intently into John's eyes.

"I will, Mrs. Parkes," John assured her. "I promise."

Georgia gave him a hug. "Thanks for being a good friend."

"You're welcome," John said awkwardly.

Principal Vernon dismissed John and Rena to their classes as he escorted Flynn's parents to the main entrance to the school.

When Rena got to math class, Mr. Hawkings was writing math formulas on the board. Rena's mind wandered in a fog as the minutes flew by, lost in her own thoughts. *Maybe Miss Hopper would let me make flyers to put up around town,* she pondered.

The bell rang and she ran to her locker to grab her drumsticks for band class. She went to her snare drums in the back of the class as Mr. Anders handed out sheet music.

"We're going to practice some new material," Mr. Anders informed the class as he stood behind his podium. "It's called 'Stars and Stripes Forever' by John Philip Sousa."

The students read over the sheet music as Mr. Anders explained the mood of the piece, and when he finished, he asked them to play a couple of measures.

Rena's body played the drums, but her mind drifted into a daydream. She recalled the first day of eighth-grade band class. Nervously, she opened the door to the auditorium and heard the sound of instruments tuning up. There was the sound of the B-flat tones of the clarinets and the C tones of the saxophones. Her classmates were trying to hit the perfect pitch. Rena walked to the back of the class and tested her drum. It sounded out of tune, so she tightened the tension rod with her key until she had the right sound.

The music teacher had them play "The Solitary Dancer" by Warren Benson, and Rena's anxiety grew. Everyone picked up the song except her. Halfway through, she couldn't figure out the syncopated beats and terror seized her brain. Luckily for Rena, Flynn stumbled through the door barely holding onto his baritone sax. The students stopped playing, giggled, and pointed at Flynn as the music teacher briefly scolded him for being late and interrupting the class. The teacher returned to conducting the music while Flynn sat down a couple rows in front of Rena. He glanced over his shoulder and gave Rena a meek smile.

"Hold on. *Stop!*" Mr. Anders shouted to the class.

Rena snapped back to the present moment.

"Rena, you're doing your own thing again," Mr. Anders pointed to Rena and shook his head. "You're offbeat and you have this quirky rhythm going on. Slow down and read the music," he directed her as he clapped his hand to the beat.

"Sorry, Mr. Anders," Rena replied faintly. "I'm a little distracted today."

She struggled with the band teacher. Whenever he corrected her style, she felt like a robot instead of "feeling" the music.

"Focus," Mr. Anders insisted.

"OK," Rena replied, feeling the pressure. "I'll try harder."

"Rena, you look like Animal from the Muppets when you play the drums," Ruben joked, almost dropping his trombone.

The band class burst into laughter at Ruben's joke. Rena shot Ruben an evil stare. She wanted to throw a drumstick at him, but she didn't want detention for letting his foolishness bother her.

"Enough, everyone," Mr. Anders regained control over his class. "Let's try again from the top."

Rena concentrated on the sheet music but could barely keep up with her classmates. Fortunately, as the students began growing tired of practicing, the bell rang. They placed their instruments back into their band lockers and poured out of the room.

Mr. Anders pulled Rena aside to talk to her privately.

"You have a lot of talent young lady, but I'm concerned," Mr. Anders said with a furrowed brow. "Don't get distracted, and instead focus on the music. You've come a long way, so don't fall back into childlike ways. Be disciplined. I know you can do this."

"Thank you. I'll try harder." She gave him a look of determination.

Rena dropped her drumsticks off at her locker before heading to her next class. All day long, she thought about Flynn. She wondered where he had gone and hoped he wasn't hurt. The day dragged on, but she made it through English, lunch, chemistry and history.

While walking to art class, she grabbed John in the hall and mentioned her idea about making flyers.

"Good idea." John nodded.

As they entered the art room, Rena and John pulled Miss Hopper aside.

"Did Principal Vernon tell you Flynn went missing?" Rena asked.

"Yes, he did," Miss Hopper said with a concerned look on her face. "I'm worried about him."

"Me too," John confessed.

"Can John and I make flyers so we can put them up around town?" Rena asked.

"Sure," Miss Hopper said enthusiastically. "Go to the library. They have a computer, printer, and copier."

"Thanks, Miss Hopper."

⌒◞

In the library, John headed straight for the computer and typed up a flyer. Rena found a middle school yearbook and flipped through the pages until she found a picture of Flynn. She scanned the picture and saved the image onto the school's computer network. She walked over to John who was finishing up the flyer.

"Did you find a picture?" John asked.

"Yep," Rena replied.

John searched for the image on the network.

"Is this it?" John asked, pointing to a .jpeg file.

"Yes," Rena responded.

John inserted Flynn's image into the flyer. After Rena proofread it, John printed fifty copies. The school bell rang and they headed to their lockers.

"I have to go to my mom's work and see how late I can stay out," Rena told John.

"Yeah," John replied. "I'll ask Coach Blake if I can skip practice, then I'll call my parents to let them know what's going on."

"Where do you want to meet?" Rena asked.

John thought for a moment. "How about Nighthawk's Café?"

"Good idea," Rena agreed. "I'll meet you there after I talk to my mom."

"OK, see ya," John replied.

Outside Nighthawk's Café, Rena stood next to a large picture window with jade-green tiles at the base. She gazed through the window and saw a blond waiter dressed in a white coat and cap; he stood behind a curved countertop making coffee. Miss Hopper, wearing a red blouse, sat alone on a stool in front of the cherry-wood counter. She turned around and beckoned Rena to come in.

"Hi, Miss Hopper!" Rena called out as she entered the cafe.

"Hi, Rena!" Miss Hopper responded with surprise. "How's the search going?"

"I haven't started. I'm waiting for John to get here."

"I hope Flynn is OK," Miss Hopper said, a worried look on her face.

"Me too," Rena replied. She looked around and asked, "Are you here by yourself?"

"I'm waiting for someone, but I don't think he's going to show up," Miss Hopper confessed.

"I'm sorry," Rena replied, feeling a little awkward by her teacher's honesty.

"No, it's OK. I don't like eating by myself at home," Miss Hopper replied, giving Rena a lonely smile. "Even if the restaurant is empty, a waiter keeps me company."

Just then, Rena felt sorry for Miss Hopper. Her teacher seemed like a nice person and none of the students disliked her, but she ate her meals alone. A thought hit Rena like a ton of bricks. *Does anyone like me? I never get asked out on dates or invited to parties.* Her thoughts were interrupted by the sound of knocking on glass. Rena turned around and saw John standing outside the café, waving.

"John's here so I better go," Rena said. "Do you want to help look for Flynn too?"

"No." Miss Hopper let out a long sigh. "I'm going to order dinner and wait around for a while just in case."

"OK," Rena said. "See you tomorrow."

"Bye, Rena."

Rena hurried out to meet John who handed her some flyers.

"Are you ready?" John asked urgently.

"Yep," Rena said, feeling John's energy. "Let's go."

John and Rena bounced around Whitehall attaching flyers to electric poles and handing them out in stores and at gas stations along Colby Street. They veered left onto a side street and John stopped in his tracks when he saw Funnel Field.

"What's wrong?" Rena inquired, wondering why John stopped.

"Ahh." John thought out loud. "Sometimes Flynn and I would stop at Funnel Field. We'd talk about school and girls and stuff."

"Should we look there?" Rena suggested.

"It's worth a shot," John confirmed.

As they strolled through Funnel Field, Rena probed, "When you guys hang out, what do you talk about? Does he mention me?"

Rena didn't want to hear anything that would crush her heart.

"Sometimes," John said, without adding any details.

"Why doesn't he like me?" Rena asked, wanting to know more.

"What do you mean?" John asked. Rena's question shocked him.

"Every time I talk to him, he seems to blow me off, like he's not interested."

"Believe me," John assured her with a chuckle, "he's into you."

"He has a funny way of showing it," Rena said, a bit confused.

"Yeah, he's a little insecure."

"A little?" Rena asked, not expecting an answer.

⤳

Funnel Field was a complete mess. Paper wrappers and plastic cups were strewn everywhere, like broken toys lost and forgotten. John and Rena looked all over for Flynn, including in the baseball dugouts. But there was no sign of him. As Rena walked through the park feeling discouraged, John stopped to pick something up off the trampled grass.

"Rena," John said. His face lit up and his hands shook. He handed her a piece of paper. Looking down she saw a pencil drawing of herself.

"What's this?" she asked, totally confused.

"Flynn drew it in art class yesterday while you were giving your report," John said. "It must've fallen out of his pocket."

"What? Really? Flynn was here!" Rena exclaimed. "We need to tell his parents."

They ran to Flynn's parents' house, located a few blocks from Funnel Field. As they approached the house, Rena noticed a police car parked in the driveway. They ran up the porch steps, and Rena knocked on the front door.

After a few moments, Georgia opened the door and asked, "Did you find Flynn?"

"No," Rena sputtered, barely catching her breath. "But we found something that belonged to Flynn."

"Really? Please come in." Georgia Parkes welcomed them into her home. "Follow me."

Inside the dining room, Rena saw a tall detective with brown hair and broad shoulders sitting at the table with Ray. The detective had a note pad filled with notes.

"This is Rena and John." Georgia made the introduction. "They're Flynn's friends from school."

"Hi, I'm Detective Winslow." He gave them a wave.

"They found something," Georgia said, looking to Rena.

"Yes," Rena announced once she regained her breath. She handed Flynn's drawing to the detective. "Flynn drew this the other day at school."

"Where did you find this?" Detective Winslow asked somberly.

"In Funnel Field," John added.

The detective looked over the image for a moment and then handed it to Georgia.

"He really captured your features." Georgia was impressed. "I think he found his muse."

Rena bowed her head and blushed.

"Looks like he stopped by the circus last night," Winslow speculated. "Maybe he went home with a friend, ran away with the circus, or he was kidnapped. This is a good lead."

Georgia tensed up when the detective uttered the word "kidnapped". She tapped her fingers on the table and held back her emotions. Her eyes teared up again. Ray placed his hand on her shoulder, but her only response was a cold stare.

"Well, folks, you gave me plenty of information," Winslow assured them. "I'll take a ride to the next city and talk to the owner of the traveling circus. I already sent out an Amber Alert."

"Please do your very best to find my son," Georgia begged.

"I will, Mrs. Parkes," Winslow reassured her. "I set up a team to look for him, and I'll call you if we find anything. If you think of anything else, here is my number." He handed everyone business cards.

"OK," Ray said and shook the detective's hand.

Detective Winslow packed his things into his briefcase and waved his good-byes.

Rena noticed the clock on the wall read 6:50 p.m. and indicated, "I need to get home."

"Do you guys need a ride?" Ray offered.

"Sure," both Rena and John replied at the same time.

⌒⌒

Rena and John jumped into the backseat of a four door car while Georgia sat in front. Rena gave Ray directions to her home; after that everyone remained quiet for several minutes.

"John, did Flynn say anything to you?" Ray asked, breaking the silence. "Was he upset or angry about something?"

"No," John replied. "Not really. Just the usual stuff."

"What usual stuff?" Georgia pried.

"Oh." John gulped really hard. "Like 'My dad won't let me learn how to drive. My parents don't like me drawing all the time. My dad keeps lecturing me about what to take in college.' Stuff like that."

"See?" Georgia slapped Ray's arm. "I told you!"

"Sorry, Mr. Parkes," John said quietly.

"So you're saying this is all my fault?" Ray was becoming upset again and made quick glances at his wife as he drove. "You want him to go to college or not?"

"Yes," Georgia responded sternly. "But we should let him choose what to study in college. Do you want to push him away?"

"No! Rrrrggh," Ray grunted as the back of his neck turned bright red.

Rena could tell Ray was torn inside. Feeling uncomfortable, she glanced at John. She wanted out of the car before the argument between Flynn's parents escalated.

The sun had set and the darkened sky had created looming shadows on the perfectly landscaped yard by the time Rena arrived home. The porch lights reflected off the blades of grass.

Rena thanked Flynn's parent's for the ride as she jumped out of the car and closed the door.

"You're welcome," Mr. Parkes called out the car window as he drove away.

Rena quickly ran up the porch steps and opened the front door. Inside her home, she looked to her left and saw her parents sitting at the dining room table. Her mom was crying uncontrollably. Her dad's elbows rested on the table, his hands covering his face. A stack of bills were strewn across the table.

"What's wrong?" Rena asked in a trembling voice.

"We're broke." Mr. Gainsborough groaned. "All our money is gone."

10

~

Wednesday morning…

Flynn found himself lying on the dressing room floor in the circus tent. He looked around and saw a dresser in the corner of the room. The drawers were open, as if someone had been searching through their memories for answers. Flynn stood up and walked over to investigate the top drawer, only to find a violin. In the second drawer, he found the drawing of Rena. Carefully, he folded it and placed it into his back pocket for safekeeping. Closing the upper drawers, he peered inside the bottom drawer, finding nothing more than a puddle of water. A bubble formed and popped. Like an underground spring, the water rose higher, swelled over the sides of the drawer, and poured onto the ground. The water gripped Flynn's feet like quicksand, pulled him to the floor, and swallowed his body. His heart exploded with fear as his lungs tightened.

Suddenly, the semitruck stopped but Flynn's body continued moving forward. His shoulder slammed into the back of the rabbit cage, and then he jolted awake from the vivid dream. His mind was in dress rehearsal, but his body gave him a jolt into reality.

Marcel flung open the truck's back door, revealing a dark sky.

"Where are we?" Flynn asked. He rubbed his sleepy eyes. Sweat dripped off his forehead.

"Grand River," Marcel grumbled, clearly in a bad mood.

"Did I do something wrong?" Flynn inquired cautiously.

"You act like a wounded rabbit so Cordelia feels sorry for you and stays mad at me. Take the rhino to the lake so he can drink."

Marcel let Flynn out of the cage, placed a handcuff on his wrist, and attached the other end to a chain. He pulled Flynn by the chain, wrapped the chain around the rhino's body, and locked it with a padlock. Unfortunately, Flynn had only a few feet of wiggle room between the padlock and the rhino's midsection.

Marcel walked away and barked, "When you're done, bring the rhino to me."

Flynn didn't know what do, so he peered through the dark, eerie mist. He saw a lake a few yards away.

Flynn tapped the rhino's belly and said, "Are you thirsty? Come on, let's get something to drink."

The rhino blinked his massive brown eyes. He shook his head and bumped his horn into Flynn's back. Its strength almost knocked Flynn off his feet.

"Why are you making this difficult?" Flynn demanded.

The rhino stomped his foot in protest. Flynn leaned up against the beast and pushed the rhino toward the lake, but it didn't budge. With both hands, Flynn grabbed the chain and leaned back. He tried to pull, but the animal held its ground as if Flynn was made of paper. He heard Sammy and Buster chuckle. He looked over his shoulder and saw them unloading food from a nearby semitruck.

"Here!" Buster shouted as he threw a garbage bag at Flynn's head.

Flynn caught the bag and opened it up to find leaves.

"What do you want me to do with this?" he called out.

Buster laughed. "He responds better to food."

Flynn nodded, then extended a handful of fresh leaves to the rhino and asked, "Do you want something to eat?"

The animal sniffed the plants and took a few bites. Flynn threw the next handful on the ground as the rhino lumbered forward. Before the rhino stomped into the lake for a drink, Flynn kicked off his shoes.

Flynn yelped in pain as the handcuff twisted around his wrist. The rhino dragged him deeper into the lake. Flynn called for help, but his foot slipped on the murky bottom and he plunged into the abyss. Before he could swim to the surface, the rhino's knee slammed against his forehead. Instantly, Flynn's head ached and his mind was in a fog. His lungs filled with cold water; they burned and felt like they would explode. Slipping through the darkness, a long fishtail flashed in front of his blurry eyes. The tail slammed against the chain, breaking it into several pieces. Fragments of metal sank to the bottom of the lake. Flynn felt detached from his body as everything floated in slow motion. His mind faded from consciousness and his body went limp.

Flynn opened his eyes and saw Cordelia giving him chest compressions. Coughing up water, he gasped for air. Slowly regaining his composure, he propped himself up on his elbows along the bank of the lake. He looked down at her mermaid tail spread out like a Chinese fan. Instead of legs, she had an elliptical torso covered with smooth green scales. Quickly, he looked away when he realized she was naked.

Why did Cordelia save me? Flynn thought.

"Can you hand me a towel?" Cordelia blushed and pointed to a tree branch.

Flynn ran on wobbly knees to the tree and returned with the towel.

"Thanks… for… saving… me," Flynn said out of breath and handed her the towel.

"You're welcome," she replied and wrapped the towel around her waist and chest.

Flynn felt defensive, unsure if she might be a friend or a foe. *Does she support her dad or agree with her grandfather?* He felt torn between two emotions.

For a few moments, neither of them talked. Instead, they listened to the birds chirping and watched the dark sky transcend into a soft yellow glow. A white swan drifted on the lake and a dragonfly landed on Cordelia's shoulder. Flynn glanced down at her fishtail. Now that she was out of the water and the sun was beginning to rise, the fish scales slid under her pale skin and her tail slowly transformed into two long legs.

"Never seen a mermaid?" Cordelia asked, breaking the silence.

Flynn shook his head. "I thought your tail was fake."

"You're talking to a real girl with a real fishtail," she joked.

Marcel ran over to the lake and shot Flynn an angry glare. "What the heck are you doing, kid, trying to get yourself killed?"

"Hellllooo?" Cordelia interrupted. "We're talking here."

Marcel awkwardly stared at Cordelia's partially clothed body. His face turned red and he covered his eyes.

"Sorry, Cordelia, is this kid bothering you?" Marcel asked sheepishly.

Cordelia stood up, glanced over her shoulder, and said, "No, he isn't bothering me at all."

As Cordelia scurried away, Flynn again noticed that she had a slight limp, as if she was in pain.

Marcel removed the handcuffs from Flynn's wrist, then grabbed him by the collar and snarled, "I'm hungry. Follow me."

The coolness of the night still hung in the air and Flynn felt chilled in his soaked clothes. The hair on his neck bristled as he walked behind Marcel. Flynn saw several campers and semitrucks parked along the lake. In front of the trucks were a couple of picnic tables and two camping stoves. Buster stood at one stove making oatmeal, and Sammy flipped pancakes at the other. Several circus employees, including Jack, were sitting at the tables eating their breakfast. Flynn grabbed a plate of food and sat down next to Marcel.

With a mouth full of food, Jack pointed to Salvatore's motor home and indicated, "He wants to talk to you."

"Why?" Flynn inquired while stuffing his wet socks in his pocket and putting his shoes on his bare feet.

"He probably wants to fire you because you screw up every job," Marcel sneered jokingly.

Jack waved good-bye and jested, "Nice knowing you kid."

"Leave him alone." Buster defended Flynn. "He didn't do anything to you."

Flynn grabbed his plate and walked over to the motor home. With his free hand, he knocked on the door.

"Come in! The door is open," Salvatore yelled.

Flynn opened the door and stepped inside. He saw Salvatore sitting at the dining room table.

"You wanted to see me?" Flynn asked, a slight hesitation in his voice.

Salvatore pointed to an empty chair and commanded him to sit down.

Flynn cautiously walked over and sat down.

"So, you're not good with animals." Salvatore interrogated Flynn while they ate their breakfast.

Flynn shrugged his shoulders and shoveled food into his mouth.

"Jack doesn't need your help anymore. What kind of jobs have you done before?"

"I've never had a job," Flynn responded in between bites. "I go to school and I have chores."

"What are you good at?" Salvatore threw up his hands. "Do you have any skills?"

Flynn didn't want to shrink back into his turtle shell, but he couldn't think of anything to say.

"I've never thought about it," Flynn muttered. His stomach growled.

"You have no job experience, you have no skills. How are you going to pay off your debt to me? Kid, you better learn a trade, or you're not going to get ahead in this world."

Flynn dropped his fork and stared at his plate; Salvatore's lecture reminded Flynn of his father.

Salvatore continued to prod. "What classes are you good at in school?"

Flynn's ears perked up and he said, "I can draw."

"You can draw," Salvatore mimicked. "I hate to break it to you, kid, but there isn't any money in art. I have no need for…"

Before he could finish his sentence, the door slammed in the other room.

"Cordelia, is that you?" Salvatore called out.

Flynn turned around and saw Albert entering the room.

"Someone told me you did a private show for a family and erased my memory last night." Albert said, getting straight to the point.

"They're lying to you," Salvatore said, pretending to be shocked. "Why would I do that? Who told you I erased your memory?"

"A little bird," Albert said, trying to sound naïve.

"I bet Paula lied to you," Salvatore was taking a guess. "She doesn't like me. Maybe I should clip her wings."

"You better not." Albert pleaded. "She didn't do anything wrong."

"Maybe I should get rid of the kid too?"

"No, no, no!" Albert protested. "You're not firing anybody."

"Fine!" Salvatore had succeeded at manipulating his father. "Paula can stay, but you need to find a job for Flynn. I have no use for him. He says he's good at art."

Albert rubbed his mustache. "He can draw advertisement posters."

"OK, you're the boss," Salvatore said, pretending to give up his authority.

"No more private shows!" Albert shook his fist at Salvatore. "This is your last warning."

Flynn felt Salvatore's heavy stare. He knew Salvatore had used him to sidetrack his father.

Albert took a few deep breaths and regained his composure as Flynn quickly finished the last bite of his breakfast. He didn't want to stick around for the next argument.

"Walk with me," Albert invited Flynn in a comforting voice.

Salvatore grinned as Flynn and Albert left the motor home.

Flynn didn't say a word as he followed Albert to his camper, but his mind was spinning.

Before Flynn could speak, Albert apologized, "I'm sorry."

Flynn walked beside Albert in silence, unsure of how to respond to the apology.

"I don't know why Salvatore is so angry and mean to everyone," Albert continued. "He's ruthless, but I didn't teach him that." Albert didn't wait for a response from Flynn. "I told him that when I die, he'd inherit the circus. But as I get older, he keeps taking over more and more, doing as he pleases. I don't like the way he is running it now because he manipulates everyone."

As they stepped inside Albert's camper, Flynn saw antique furniture, black and white photographs of circus acts, and a stack of books sitting on a coffee table. Albert sat down in a chair next to the kitchen table, but before he could speak, Marcel opened the camper door.

Albert pointed a boney finger at Marcel and said, "Don't you know how to knock?"

"Salvatore told me to keep an eye on the kid." Marcel defended his intrusion.

"Fine." Albert shrugged his shoulders.

Marcel started to sit down in a chair, but Albert snapped, "What are you doing?"

Marcel looked around the room and replied, "Sitting down."

"Get some poster board and pencils," Albert commanded. "We need some drawing material so Flynn can draw advertisement posters for our circus."

"OK," Marcel snapped bitterly, slamming the door as he left.

Flynn found his opportunity to talk to Albert alone. In a shaky voice Flynn said, "I need to tell you something important."

"What is it?" Albert asked, listening intently.

"I didn't come to the circus looking for a job." Flynn unloaded his burden. "Salvatore kidnapped me. I told you this before, but you forgot. Not because you have Alzheimer's. You forgot because Salvatore erased your memory."

"What? I didn't know that my son was forcing you to stay here against your will," Albert confessed. "He has gone too far this time. First, he robs people of their money, now he kidnaps you. He's out of control."

"Can you help me escape?" Flynn pleaded.

"I don't know." Albert sighed. "I'm not as strong as I used to be. Jack is Salvatore's personal bodyguard. Every time I try to stop him, Jack and the lions get in the way. Marcel, Sammy, and Buster are scared of my son, and they won't stop him from his greed. Can I trust you?"

Flynn felt the hidden courageous lion begin to grow inside. He confidently nodded his head and said, "Yes, you can trust me."

"Good." Albert said with delight. "We don't have much time. Marcel will be back soon."

"But how can I help you?" Flynn didn't understand.

"I'm not sure how, but if we're going to defeat my son, you'll need some powers," Albert explained with a smile. "I'll give you the power to change your drawings into real objects!"

11

~

"Turn drawings into reality? That's impossible!" Flynn interjected; he couldn't comprehend the possibilities.

"Nothing is impossible." Albert raised his eyebrows. "Most things you see in this world were once an idea in someone's head. Look at the Wright Brothers. People thought they were crazy when they designed an airplane, but they made flying possible. A builder builds structures using an architect's drawings. Designers make their drawings real just by printing them with a 3-D printer. You can do great things with your imagination."

Albert tapped Flynn on his head and said, "Imagination is more important than knowledge. Knowledge is limited by what we know and understand in the present moment. Imagination, on the other hand, is limitless."

Albert motioned Flynn to sit down at the kitchen table and told him to place his hands on the table with his palms up. Albert went into the kitchen and came back with a glass of water. He set it down on the table in front of Flynn. Albert lit a candle, placed it in front of the glass, then sat down at the table. He pulled out a tattered scroll from a drawer and unrolled it. He took out a small fabric bag and a pencil from his coat pocket. Secret Talent Scroll was written in bold letters at the top of the scroll.

"Are you right-handed or left?" Albert asked.

"Right-handed."

Albert placed the pencil in Flynn's right hand, then reached into the fabric bag and pulled out a few grains of sand.

Albert stared at the scroll and chanted, "I call on the four classical elements, wind, fire, earth, and water. Wind moves sand. Fire creates earth and ash. Earth absorbs water. Water quenches fire. Give Flynn the ability to change drawings from his imagination into real objects."

From an open window, a light breeze blew the sand out of Albert's hand. The sand sailed through the candle flame and turned into glowing embers, emitting sparks like a miniature fireworks show. Defying gravity, droplets of water from the glass floated up and extinguished the embers. Slowly, the embers turned into black ash and dropped onto Flynn's open palms and pencil. A tingling sensation moved from his fingers to his hands, to his forearm, and then shot past his elbow. A cool chill ran through Flynn's spine and he felt light-headed.

Suddenly, they heard a knock on the camper door. Albert quickly blew out the candle, put the bag into his pocket, drank the glass of water, and placed the scroll back inside the table drawer.

"Come in!" Albert shouted as Flynn tucked the special pencil into his pocket.

Marcel climbed inside the camper carrying two poster boards and pencils. He laid the poster board and pencils on the table.

Marcel looked at Flynn and said, "You don't look so good. You look like you've seen a ghost."

"You scare me," Flynn shivered in his seat.

Shrugging his shoulders, Marcel walked into the living room, sat in a recliner chair, and turned on the TV.

Flynn picked up a pencil and asked Albert, "What should I draw for the circus poster?"

"Hmm…" Albert pondered. "Why don't you draw a poster of Salvatore, Cordelia, and a couple of the animals? On top write an invitation to the traveling circus."

Albert took some pictures off the wall and placed them on the table next to Flynn.

"Use these photographs as a reference," Albert suggested.

One black and white photo showed Jack holding Hula-Hoops as the rabbits jumped through them. Another showed Salvatore standing on a wooden barrel as Cordelia swam in a small pool.

"When was this picture taken?" Flynn asked.

"About five years ago," Albert estimated.

"How long has Cordelia been with the circus?" Flynn ventured a question.

"All her life."

"What about your son? Why did he join the circus?"

"Salvatore excelled at math and science in school," Albert explained. "I thought he could earn a living as a scientist, so I pressured him to study physics in college. It wasn't his passion, so he dropped out after Cordelia was born. He needed money to support his family, so he came to work for me, running the circus."

Albert sighed and continued. "But he wasn't the same after dropping out of college. He was cold toward the world and me. Maybe I should've let him figure out what he wanted to do on his own."

Flynn just nodded; he could relate to the story. Then, Flynn noticed another photograph on the wall next to the kitchen table. It showed Albert and Cordelia standing on a sidewalk outside Howmet Playhouse in Whitehall. In the background of the photograph, Flynn saw himself laying on the ground with his bike! He searched his memory bank. *Did I meet Albert and Cordelia before?* Flynn thought.

"You should finish the poster," Albert said cautiously. "I don't know when Salvatore will come looking for you."

Flynn would have to save his questions for another time. He laid down the poster board on the table and started drawing. After a half an hour, Flynn dropped his pencil.

Marcel took a break from watching TV, walked over to the table, and glanced at Flynn's poster.

"Not bad, kid." Marcel nodded in approval.

Marcel grabbed a granola bar from the kitchen and slumped back into the recliner. He was easily entertained after switching to an action movie on TV.

While Marcel munched and watched the TV mindlessly, Albert whispered to Flynn, "He's distracted. You should practice your new skill. Start out with something small."

Flynn looked around the room. He saw an apple sitting in a fruit bowl and drew it.

"Now what?" Flynn asked as he set the pencil down.

"Use your imagination to make it real," Albert whispered.

Flynn concentrated on the image. To his amazement, the apple slowly pushed through the flat surface of the paper. Instead of being red, the apple was different shades of gray.

"Wow!" Flynn whispered. "I did it! I created an apple from my imagination. But why is the apple gray?"

"Because of the pencil lead," Albert speculated. "The pencil gave it shape. Use your mind to fill it with color."

Flynn nodded and focused on the apple. Slowly, the apple filled in with red and green, as if someone with an invisible brush colored its skin. It looked polished, like the fruit inside a grocery store, and Flynn grabbed it and took a bite.

"It tastes like an apple!"

"With a little practice, you can draw anything with that pencil, but don't tell anyone about your gift…not yet," Albert whispered. "For now you should make a flyer to hand out around town."

The movie ended and Marcel turned off the TV. He walked over to the table where Flynn and Albert were seated.

"I need to set up the tents," Marcel said impatiently. "Are you guys done yet?"

"Yes," Albert answered flatly.

Marcel looked at the poster and said, "Good job, kid. Now, take it to Salvatore."

Flynn nodded, gathering the poster and the flyer. Outside the camper, he saw Salvatore and Cordelia standing in front of a group of circus workers.

Salvatore pointed to an open field and gave them instructions: "I want the main tent set up back there. Then, I want you to set up the smaller tents in two rows. Place the food vendors and merchandise in between the small tents. The rides go over there. We only have a few hours before people start arriving, so we need to hustle. Let's go!"

As the workers scattered, Salvatore looked at Flynn and asked, "What have you got for me?"

Flynn held up the posters and the flyer.

Salvatore carefully looked them over. "I suppose these will do. Cordelia, take the kid into town and make copies of the flyer. On the way back, put up the posters and hand out the flyers. Can you handle that, kid?"

Flynn nodded.

"We'll be hitting forty more cities before the end of the year," Salvatore boasted. "So you'll need to create a lot more posters."

"Marcel!" Salvatore looked around and shouted. "Where are you? I need to talk to you."

"Yes, boss?" Marcel ran up beside Salvatore like a puppy eager to make his master happy.

"Go with them into town and make sure the kid doesn't try running away," Salvatore commanded. "In my motor home are some nails and a hammer; you can use them to put up the posters."

"Aren't you worried someone will recognize the kid?" Marcel looked puzzled.

"We're in another town. He looks like any other kid," Salvatore snapped. "Who's going to recognize him?"

Marcel shrugged his shoulders with skepticism.

Marcel, Flynn and Cordelia gathered the tools from Salvatore's motor home and headed into town. Flynn and Cordelia walked side by side while Marcel, who was in his normal human size, trailed a few steps behind. Again, Cordelia appeared to shuffle along, unable to make a complete stride in her walk.

Flynn couldn't keep his eyes off of Cordelia. She looked beautiful in her green summer dress; a barrette held back her curly red hair. Flynn noticed a tarnished locket hanging around her neck. He stared a second too long, and she caught him staring at her.

"Is something wrong?" Cordelia asked, looking down at her legs.

"No," Flynn responded sheepishly. "I was just looking at your locket."

"Oh…My mom gave it to me," Cordelia explained.

She stopped and opened the locket, revealing two pictures inside. One photograph was of her grandfather who looked much younger with tan hair and no wrinkles. The other picture was of her mom and dad standing together. Cordelia looked a lot like her mother; she even had the same curly red hair and green eyes.

"Your mom is very pretty," Flynn complimented her as they continued walking down the sidewalk. "You look just like her."

"Thanks," Cordelia said modestly as she closed the locket.

"Where's your mom now?" Flynn asked cautiously.

Cordelia bit her lip. "She's gone."

"Gone?" Flynn was perplexed. "Where?"

"In high school, I was on a swim team. I loved the water, and I practiced every day because my dream was to qualify for the Olympics." As Cordelia told her story, her radiant face turned gray and the bounce in her step slowed. "My mom was my biggest supporter. She did everything and anything for me. One day, when my mom drove me to practice, someone ran a red light and smashed into the car." Cordelia exhaled deeply and turned her head away.

"My mom..." Cordelia choked up. "She was killed on impact. I broke my ankles and wrecked my knees. They never healed properly, and now I walk with a limp. The pain is a reminder of what I lost. Everything I loved vanished that day."

Overwhelmed by the tragic story, Flynn stopped in his tracks. He noticed the tears in her eyes as her bright-green eyes slowly dimmed.

"So that's why Albert turned you into a mermaid, so you could swim again?" Flynn felt compelled to ask.

"Yes," she said sadly.

Flynn watched her wipe away her tears.

"He knows I love to swim." She spoke fondly of her grandfather. "I guess it was his way of bringing back my passion in life."

Flynn took a deep breath and pondered Cordelia's story. He couldn't find the words to express his feelings, so they silently walked into town.

Grand River was a large city; it had several blocks of retail shops, and the streets were crowded with cars. They found a printing store where they could make copies of Flynn's flyer and poster.

Flynn politely opened the door for Cordelia. She asked the clerk behind the counter for a hundred copies of the flyer and fifteen of the poster. They stood awkwardly in silence as they waited for the clerk to come back with the copies. She paid in cash and they left the store.

Cordelia smiled and handed out flyers to passing pedestrians. Marcel stopped to talk to a group of kids on bikes. Flynn saw a wall near a construction site and went over to nail a poster on it; he stepped back to make sure it looked level.

An older gentleman dressed in a tweed jacket stopped to look at the poster.

"Did you draw this?" the man quizzed Flynn.

"Yes, I did."

"You have some potential for your age," the man said with a look of surprise. "Have you thought about going to an art college?"

"Sometimes." Flynn shrugged his shoulders. "But my parents would never pay for it."

The man took out his wallet and handed Flynn a business card that read "Professor Copley, Grand River Art College."

"I teach graphic art classes at the college," Copley said. "If you put together a portfolio, maybe we can meet and I'll take a look at it? We offer degrees in fine art, graphic design and furniture design. I think you could be a great fit for our school. You may even qualify for a scholarship."

Overwhelmed by a sudden rush of excitement at the positive feedback, Flynn didn't know what to say. "Thank you!" he managed.

The man shook Flynn's hand before continuing on his way. Flynn stuffed the business card into his jean pocket just as Cordelia and Marcel finished talking to the kids. Marcel looked at Flynn as the professor walked away.

"Who was that?" Marcel asked angrily.

"Not sure." Flynn lied. "He just said 'I like the poster.'"

"What did you say to him?" Marcel demanded furiously.

"Nothing, I swear." Flynn didn't want to divulge any more information.

Marcel grabbed Flynn by the shirt and dragged him across the street. People on the street stared as Cordelia chased after them, but nobody stopped or bothered to say anything. With fury in his eyes, Marcel pushed Flynn into an alley between two buildings and threw him behind a dumpster. Flynn bounced off the wall and fell to the ground. His knee slammed into the pavement, ripping his pants at the knee. Blood trickled from his wound. Flynn felt a sharp pain in his knee as he stood up and leaned against the brick wall.

"Did you tell him about the circus and Salvatore?" Marcel barked. "Did you tell him to call the police?"

Marcel's strength and anger caused Flynn's heart to beat furiously.

"I didn't say anything," Flynn pleaded. "I swear!"

Marcel punched Flynn in the stomach, knocking the wind out of him. Flynn doubled over in pain.

Cordelia ran up behind Marcel and yelled, "Don't hurt him! He's telling the truth."

Marcel picked Flynn up off the ground. His shirt ripped as his biceps grew in size. Flynn's feet dangled in the air.

Marcel snarled, "You better not be lying to me."

Cordelia stood behind Marcel and placed her hand on his shoulder. Her presence calmed him slightly.

"I believe him," she said honestly. "I don't think he said anything."

Marcel looked at Cordelia, then at Flynn. He let go of his shirt, dropping him to the ground. Flynn looked up at Marcel as he sat on his hands and knees.

"If that guy goes to the police," Marcel warned as he walked away, "I'll give you a beating you'll never forget."

Flynn felt a lump in his throat.

Cordelia looked at Flynn's ripped jeans, kneeled down and asked, "Are you OK?"

"I'll be all right," Flynn assured her.

Cordelia placed her hand under Flynn's elbow and helped him up. He walked with a slight limp, thanks to the throbbing pain in his knee.

"We've a lot ground to cover," Marcel grumbled impatiently. "So let's go. Flynn, don't talk anymore people and stay close to me."

Flynn nodded.

They walked up and down the sidewalks, handing out flyers. Flynn's knee stung with pain and he avoided eye contact with Marcel. He hid his limp from Marcel, not wanting to give him the satisfaction of knowing he was hurt. By the time they had handed out all the flyers and hung up the last poster, it was close to show time, so they quietly walked back to the fairgrounds. Soon Flynn would realize it was the calm before the storm.

12

~

Flynn, Cordelia, and Marcel arrived back at the fairgrounds just before opening time. The fairgrounds looked busy with workers running every which way, setting up the tents and scrubbing the covers with brooms. Vendors unloaded boxes of souvenirs from the semitrucks and cleaned the food cart windows. Jack and Salvatore were talking in front of the main tent.

"Marcel!" Jack shouted when he saw them enter the park. "Could you give me a hand?"

"Cordelia," Marcel pointed to Flynn and requested, "could you watch him for me?"

"Sure," Cordelia said as Marcel scurried away.

Out of the corner of his eye, Flynn noticed Salvatore was strutting over to them.

"I fired Paula," Salvatore stated without remorse. "So I need Flynn to fill that position."

"What? I don't know how to be a trapeze artist."

Ignoring Flynn's comment, Salvatore looked at his daughter and asked, "Can you take him to the dressing room and find him a costume?"

Cordelia gave her father a nod and led Flynn to a camper that contained the circus performers' accessories. Inside the camper, Flynn saw a variety of colorful costumes, ranging from clown outfits to trapeze jumpsuits. Everything smelled musty and stale.

"Have a seat," she said, pulling his eyes away from the costumes and back to her. "I'll sew up your ripped jeans."

Flynn sat down in a empty chair; he felt a little more comfortable around her now.

"My mom taught me a lot, including sewing and making lace." Cordelia opened up to Flynn.

"That's cool," Flynn replied as Cordelia pushed a stool in front his chair. She set a blue pillow on top of the stool so Flynn could rest his wounded leg.

She placed gauze and a strip of tape around his wound before focusing intently on mending the rip in his pant leg.

"I'm glad we ditched Marcel," she said, trying not to poke him with the needle.

"Me too," Flynn agreed. "I can't believe he punched me. He says it's my fault you don't like him."

Her hand twitched at Flynn's comment; the needle grazed his knee.

"Ouch!" Flynn flinched.

"I'm sorry." Cordelia rubbed his calf. "Marcel makes me mad, but that's not your fault."

"Why does he make you mad?" Flynn wanted to know the story.

Cordelia hesitated for a moment, and then she explained. "When my dad hired Marcel, I kind of liked him, you know... I thought he was cute. He used to hang around my pool after he was done with the circus. He acted nice and I thought maybe we could become more than just friends."

"So what happened?" Flynn asked.

"One day, I asked him if he wanted to see my aquarium," Cordelia continued, her demeanor now turning tense, her lips tightening. "He said 'OK' so we went to my trailer and I showed him all the fish. Without warning, he grabbed my shoulders and started to kiss me. I pushed him away and asked him to stop, but he kept kissing me anyway."

Cordelia turned her head away, embarrassed by the story.

Despite the lump that had formed in his throat, Flynn asked, "Then what?"

"Jack knocked on the door because he needed Marcel's help. Marcel left my camper, and I haven't talked about it since."

"Why didn't you tell your dad?"

"Because I knew what my dad would do to him," Cordelia expressed her feelings with a tear in her eye. "He's way over protective. He would destroy Marcel's memory. Imagine learning everything all over again. Relying on other people for help. I couldn't do that to Marcel. So I pushed him away. I know he still likes me, but..." Her voice trailed off.

"I'm sorry." Flynn didn't know what else to say.

"I don't want to talk about Marcel anymore," Cordelia said and changed the subject. "How did my dad convince you to work for us?"

"I thought he told you."

"No," she shook her head. "We don't talk much. He's too busy running the circus."

Her denial surprised him. "As the circus closed," Flynn explained, "I saw your dad talk to someone from my school. So I followed them into the main tent, and I got caught watching a private show. Your dad said I needed to repay him for watching."

"Nothing in life is free," Cordelia said flatly with a frown. She didn't seem surprised by her dad's actions; she acted as if she condoned them.

Her remark surprised Flynn. He hesitated to ask her another personal question, but he needed to know.

"Most of the money your dad makes comes from the private performances." Flynn replied. "Do you know that's where he gets your jewelry too?"

Cordelia's frown turned into a scowl. "We work hard to entertain people," she said, crossing her arms. "Marcel, Jack, and I are special. We deserve to be rewarded for our talents."

Suddenly, Flynn felt the tension in the air. He should've never brought up the stolen jewelry.

Cordelia finished sewing up the rip in his jeans and then handed him a helmet.

"You're going to need this," she warned him as she handed him a costume. "When you're done changing your clothes, come and get me."

Flynn reluctantly nodded.

After Cordelia left him alone inside the camper, Flynn began to contemplate his escape. He pulled back the curtain and saw Marcel a few yards away from the camper. If he ran for the exit, Marcel might chase him down. He needed another plan, something more than running away.

Maybe I should draw a gun? No, Flynn thought, *I could never shoot anybody. I don't even know how to use a gun. Maybe I could draw someone and they can go to the police.*

Flynn locked the camper door and found a blank wall. The first person who popped into his mind was Rena. She was never far removed from his thoughts. He could recall every detail of her radiant face. Since he had drawn her in art class, he wouldn't have any trouble drawing her again. Using his memory, he sketched Rena's feet and legs, tracing up to her fingers, hands, and arms. Then he drew her face, hair, and ears. He took a few steps backward, but nothing happened. *Maybe I can't draw people, only objects?* he thought. He added a few more details to Rena's eyes and stepped back to admire the picture.

Flynn felt her presence calm his nerves even though she was so far away. Then he heard the paint crack and the drywall crumble. Rena's image rippled like waves on a lake as two hands and her feet pushed through the wall. She fell to the floor, covered in white dust and plasterboard. Flynn's drawing folded space, created a pocket in time, and Rena appeared inside the trailer. He brushed the dust off her. Startled and confused, she looked up at Flynn and then around the room.

"Where am I?" she asked in a bewildered voice. "How did I get here?"

Before he could answer, she rattled off a ton of information. "Your parents came to school and talked to John. We searched all over town for you. My parents lost all their money. And a police detective is looking for you!"

"Rena, shh! Just listen."

He briefly explained what had happened in the last two days. He talked about the rabbits turning into lions and how Salvatore had stolen her family's money. He told her about being kidnapped by Salvatore and how Albert had given him the power to turn drawings into real objects.

Rena paced the floor and contemplated all the information.

"Why didn't you draw a picture of a cell phone and call the cops?" Rena finally asked.

"Darn it!" Flynn slapped his forehead. "You're right. Why didn't I think of that? I'm so sorry I got you into this mess."

Rena put her hand up and said, "It's OK. I'm glad you thought of me. What now?"

"I have a plan. You're going to hide in the trailer. When the gates open to the public, you can sneak out of the park and go to the police. Tell them I was kidnapped and where they can find me. Can you help me?"

"Yes, but my clothes," Rena said. "They're paper thin and they look... well, they look kinda like a cartoon."

"You're right," Flynn said; he noticed her clothes were thin as paper.

They heard a loud knock on the camper door.

"Quick, hide!" Flynn whispered.

Danger lurked everywhere, and they needed to act fast. So he gently pushed Rena into the clothes closet. It was the first time he had touched her since the eighth-grade dance. A few days ago, the thought of touching her had caused him to seize up with anxiety. Calamity now forced him out of his shell of self-doubt, and the warmth of her body felt magical.

Rena hid in the closet while he pushed the broken drywall crumbs under a rug.

"Come in!" Flynn shouted.

"Are you dressed?" Cordelia yelled from outside the camper. "My dad's mad. He said you're taking too long."

"Sorry. I'm almost dressed," Flynn responded. "I feel silly wearing a jump suit. What if people make fun of me?"

Cordelia peered inside the camper and impatiently said, "You look fine. Let's go."

Struggling to put on the trapeze shoes, Flynn followed Cordelia to the main tent. As he glanced back at the camper, he hoped Rena wouldn't get caught and that they'd get home safely.

"Come on!" Cordelia prodded.

Inside the tent, Flynn asked Salvatore defiantly, "What do you want me to do now?"

"Tonight we're putting on a private performance for a very lucky family," Salvatore replied, pointing to a cannon.

"Lucky?" Flynn snipped. "No one feels lucky when they're being robbed."

Salvatore swelled with anger and spouted, "What did you say? Mind your tongue, kid. I see a rabbit, not a lion, standing in front of me!"

Knowing he needed to buy time for Rena, Flynn asked, "What do you want me to do?"

"We're practicing a routine without Paula," Salvatore informed him. "We're going to shoot you from the cannon, and Rego is going to catch you."

Pointing to Rego on a high platform, Salvatore said, "Hurry up. Rego is waiting."

Salvatore walked over to the bleachers and sat down.

Rego climbed down the trapeze ladder and came over to Flynn.

"Any pointers?" Flynn asked.

"Keep your body straight and your eyes focused on me," Rego explained. "It's all about timing. Before grabbing my hands, slow your momentum by stretching out your arms and legs. Place your arms and hands over your head just as you're getting close to me. You won't get a net for the show. Salvatore doesn't care if you get hurt. It's like a car wreck—the audience can't help but look. And, unfortunately, Salvatore sees this as a way to turn tragedy into money."

"Will anyone catch me if I fall?" Flynn asked hopefully.

"I'll try, but there's no guarantee," Rego replied. "So you better get it right. Sorry, kid. Enough talking. We should practice."

Flynn realized this was a sink-or-swim moment. He could either give up or fight for survival. *I'm going to take charge of my life,* Flynn thought.

He saw Buster add more gunpowder to the cannon, smiling all giddy as he prepared the cannon for ignition. While hanging from his knees and upside down, Rego swung back and forth on the trapeze bar.

Flynn stepped up to the cannon, replaying Rego's instructions over and over in his mind. Out of the corner of his eye, he saw Albert walk into the main tent and sit down in the bleachers. Flynn felt nervous, but he had no choice. He focused on success and remembered Albert's advice: *Never let shyness or fear over power you.*

As Flynn crawled inside the barrel of the cannon, Buster said, "On the count of three, I'll light the fuse." He counted down, "Three, two, one, ignition!"

KA-BOOM!

Keeping his body straight and his eyes locked on Rego, Flynn launched into the air. The air rushing past his face made his eyes water. Flynn stretched out his arms and legs, which slowed him down slightly. He placed his arms over his head and felt both his hands connect with Rego's. With their hands in a tight grip, their bodies swung back and forth.

With a sense of accomplishment, Flynn shouted, "I did it!"

After a few swings, Rego said, "I think you got the hang of this. Grab onto the platform."

Flynn released one hand from Rego's grip and grabbed onto the platform bar, then he did the same with his other hand. As he pulled himself up to the platform, one hand slipped. His body twisted and almost pulled his other hand free from the platform. Keeping his composure, he shifted his weight, swung his arm around, and grabbed the platform with both hands. He pulled himself onto the platform and climbed down the ladder.

Albert clapped, walked over to Flynn and shook his hand.

"Good job!" Albert congratulated him. "Once you have positive thoughts about yourself, anything is possible."

"Thanks!" Flynn said, smiling in appreciation.

"I haven't seen you in a few hours," Albert whispered. "I thought maybe you'd escaped."

In a hushed tone, Flynn replied, "No, but I have plan. I drew someone from school and..."

Flynn didn't have time to finish his sentence because Salvatore interrupted them.

"What are you guys talking about?"

"Nothing," Albert deflected the question. "Son, we need to talk in private."

"I don't have time," Salvatore shot back. "I have a show to run."

"Fine!" Albert stood his ground firmly. "I'm going to my tent, but we'll talk later."

"OK," Salvatore sighed, clearly annoyed with his father.

Albert stormed out of the tent.

"Buster, you're supposed to keep an eye on him!" Salvatore scolded Buster like a dog. "You had a simple task: keep Albert in the dark. If you can't handle that job, I'll find someone who can."

Buster remained silent, afraid to look into Salvatore's eyes.

"Marcel! Get in here!" Salvatore shouted.

Marcel didn't come running into the tent like a lost puppy. Salvatore wasn't used to his employees not following orders.

"Where the heck is Marcel?" Salvatore fumed. "Buster, go find Marcel and bring him in here!"

"OK, boss." Buster jumped on command and ran out of the tent. Several minutes later, Buster led Marcel back into the main tent.

"Why didn't you come running when I called for you?" Salvatore asked angrily.

"I caught some girl running away with one of our costumes," Marcel informed his boss, trying to catch his breath.

Girl? Costume? Flynn worried. *Did Marcel catch Rena?* Flynn didn't say a word.

13

~

Earlier in the camper, from Rena's eyes…

"Quick, hide!" Flynn whispered when they heard a knock on the camper door.

Rena squeezed into the closet and gagged on the smell of musty clothes and mothballs. Slowly, her eyes adjusted to the dark and she heard Flynn brushing broken drywall crumbs under a rug.

Flynn shouted, "Come in!"

A female voice replied, "Are you dressed? My dad's mad. He said you're taking too long."

Who's that girl? Rena wondered.

"Sorry. I'm almost dressed." Flynn replied. "I feel silly wearing a jump suit. What if people make fun of me?"

That's quick thinking, using his appearance for not being ready, Rena smiled to herself, noticing a new side to Flynn.

The girl responded urgently, "You look fine. Let's go."

Rena heard the camper door slam shut, and after a few minutes of silence she opened the closet door a small crack. Nervously peering into the room, she saw that it was now empty. She tiptoed to the window and slowly pushed the curtain back a few inches. She adjusted her view so she could see the whole park. Circus employees were finishing setting up the main tent, food carts, and merchandise tables. A few customers began trickling through the gates.

She couldn't go out in public with paper-thin clothes, so she looked for a costume to wear. She saw a silly jester's hat with three bells and put that on. Then she found shoes with the toes that curled up and striped green shorts with elastic to hold them firmly around her waist.

She looked out the window for the second time. More people had arrived, so she ventured outside. She didn't want to look out of place, so she skipped playfully along like a court jester. As she made her way toward an exit, she passed by a muscular man standing in front of a Strength High Striker. He entertained the crowd by slamming a sledgehammer, with one hand, against a lever. His powerful blow propelled the puck straight up the pole to hit the bell. As he turned around to accept the crowd's applause, he saw Rena. A puzzled look crossed his face.

Oh no. He knows I'm not with the circus, Rena thought nervously. She skipped faster, acting like everything was normal.

The muscular man handed the sledgehammer to a customer standing behind him.

"Hey! I've seen you before," he called out. "Where did you get that costume? Who are you? Stop!"

Her legs felt light as a feather and her feet barely touched the ground as she began to run. She never ran so fast, not even the time when she had been surprised by a hissing snake while hiking in the woods a few years back.

Glancing over her shoulder, Rena saw the man chasing her. She weaved in and out of the crowd hoping her movement would slow him down, but he wouldn't give up the chase. Just a few yards from the exit, she felt a hand grab her shirtsleeve. The man yanked so hard it stopped Rena in her tracks. Losing her balance, she spun to the ground and her sleeve ripped off at the shoulder. Paralyzed with fear, Rena looked up at the muscular man towering above her.

Oh no. I'm trapped! Rena feared. Behind the muscular man, Rena saw a clown come running out of the main tent. She heard the clown yell, "Marcel!"

The clown grabbed Marcel's elbow and shouted, "Salvatore wants to talk to you *right now!*"

"Buster! What are you doing?" Marcel scowled. "Remember this girl from the other night? She stole a costume!"

"Never mind that!" Buster said, clearly frustrated.

"Why does Salvatore need to see me *right now?*" Marcel growled.

"Someone needs to watch Flynn," Buster fired back.

"Can't you do that?" Marcel asked as he punched Buster in the shoulder.

"He wants *you* to watch him," Buster said, rubbing his sore shoulder.

Rena watched them argue and realized she almost lost her opportunity to escape. Quickly, she scrambled to her feet and ran toward the exit.

"Hey!" Marcel shouted angrily. "*Stop!*"

Rena heard Buster reply with stress in his voice. "Let her go!"

She glanced over her shoulder and noticed Marcel stomping away with Buster. *That was a close one*, Rena thought as she ran out the main gate.

Rena sprinted through town desperately looking for the police department. Her muscles ached and the air felt like sandpaper in her lungs as she gasped for oxygen, but she couldn't stop now. She didn't recognize the city or the street signs; she felt lost and alone. People gave her strange looks when they noticed her torn and dirty costume. After tossing the jester hat into a trashcan, she approached a man wearing a business suit.

"Where can I find the police station?" Rena asked, trying to catch her breath.

"Take Scribner Street to Pearl, then hang a right on Monroe. Go down a few blocks and you'll see a large building. You can't miss it," he said, gawking at her costume.

"Thanks!" Rena replied.

"No problem," he said quizzically.

Jogging west on Pearl Street, she thought about what Buster had said: "He needs *you* to watch Flynn."

Was Flynn in more danger? Was Marcel going to hurt Flynn? She pondered whether or not to go back and help. She realized she might be kidnapped too, so she continued moving. After several minutes of sprinting, she finally found the police station.

"Can someone help me?" Rena blurted out when she got to the reception desk. Her heart pounded and she breathed heavily. "My friend Flynn is in danger."

The woman at the counter didn't reply; she immediately picked up the phone and made a call. The receptionist looked up and down at Rena's outfit. A short minute later, a young woman in her midthirties rushed to the front desk. She had a gun holster on her right hip and a badge hooked onto her belt.

"I'm Officer Cassatt. Can I help you?"

"I'm Rena. My friend Flynn Parkes was kidnapped a few days ago. I found him in the park a few blocks from here."

"You mean Abner Park?"

"I think so," Rena speculated. "I can show you."

"That would be great!" Cassatt said.

"Detective Winslow, from Whitehall, has been looking for Flynn too," Rena added.

"Come with me," Cassatt requested. "I'll call him from my desk."

Rena followed the officer down a long corridor and turned a corner. The hallway opened up into a large room filled with cubicles. Many contained an officer talking on a phone or asking a witness questions. Rena took a seat at Officer Cassatt's desk while she called the Whitehall Police Department. Rena felt like she was going to burst from impatience. *Can't this wait? We need to get to Flynn*, Rena thought.

"Hello," Officer Cassatt spoke into the phone. "Yes, I would like to talk to Detective Winslow. Thanks."

"How old is Flynn?" Cassatt asked, tilting the phone away from her mouth and looking briefly at Rena. "Was he OK when you found him?"

"I think he's fifteen and he looked like he was OK," Rena answered impatiently. Her shoulders tensed up and her lips were dry. She couldn't understand why the police weren't taking quicker actions. "He just wants to go home."

Cassatt nodded.

"Hi, Detective," she said, turning her attention to the phone call. "This is Officer Cassatt from the Grand River Police Department. I'm calling about a boy named Flynn Parkes." The officer stopped in mid sentence and paused before responding with, "Whoa, hold on. I'm going to put you on speakerphone."

Cassatt pushed a red button on the phone and asked, "Are you still there?"

"Yes." Detective Winslow's voice emitted from the speaker.

"I have Rena here," Officer Cassatt explained, but Winslow interrupted her.

"Rena, where have you been? I got a desperate call from your principal; he said you disappeared from school!" His voice was full of confusion.

"I found Flynn!" Rena relayed the good news with a tense smile.

"You what? How? Where? When?" Winslow inquired. "Where is he? I can meet you there."

"It's a long story, and I can tell you when you get here," Rena asserted, trying to save valuable time. "He's still in danger."

"We think Flynn's at Abner Park," Cassatt interrupted diplomatically. "I'll set up a team of officers to retrieve him."

"Good," Winslow said, his voice calming to a normal business tone. "I'll call you when I'm on the road to get the details."

"OK," Cassatt said and gave Winslow her number. "See you soon."

Rena sat back in the chair and her shoulders slumped in relief. *Finally, Flynn will be coming home and this nightmare will be over.* Unfortunately, her relief was premature.

Officer Cassatt hung up the phone, looked at Rena, and quizzed, "Who kidnapped Flynn? Do they have any weapons?"

"Flynn said the owner of the circus kidnapped him. He has trained lions that protect him." Rena volunteered all the information she could remember from Flynn's story.

"You say lions? Well, we're going to need a tranquilizer dart gun. Is there anything else you can remember that might be helpful?" Cassatt asked.

"No." Rena pondered. "I don't think so."

"OK." Officer Cassatt gave Rena a slight nod. "Wait here. I'll let my boss know about the situation."

Rena looked around the room and noticed a lot of unhappy faces. Each one of them had a sad story to tell a police officer. Rena's foot twitched and she became nervous. *I hope we're not too late,* she worried.

14

~

Flynn and Marcel were outside, setting up props and equipment for the show. When Marcel disappeared into a small tent to get something, Flynn darted to the costume trailer and peered inside the window. Rena wasn't there. He hoped she had escaped and gotten to the police. To avoid suspicion, Flynn hurried back to work before Marcel returned.

Sammy and Buster were near the main gate where the crowd dispersed to various rides and sideshows. Sammy stood next to a cylindrical helium tank, and Buster had a basket full of deflated balloons at his feet. Sammy filled the balloons with helium while Buster twisted and bent them into different shapes. A little girl requested a flower, so Buster pinched, rolled, and twisted a green and a red balloon together to make a rose with a long stem. She smiled as Buster presented it to her. He kindly patted the girl's head, and as she left, more kids lined up to receive balloon animals.

In front of the main tent, Jack handed the end of a jump rope to a female assistant. Jack snapped his fingers and swung the long rope. On command, three rabbits hopped up and down. They performed jump rope tricks while a group of kids giggled with delight.

Salvatore stood in front of Cordelia's tent, enticing customers with a new sales pitch: "Have you ever seen a beautiful young woman with a fishtail? Do you think mermaids are just a myth? Well, step right up and for a small price you'll get to see a *real* mermaid."

Salvatore pointed to the ticket booth, and a few people stepped forward. One family strolled past Salvatore, catching his eye. The dad wore a suit, and his wife's fingernails were manicured and painted red. Their son's clothes were neatly pressed, and their daughter's hair looked as if she had just come from a hair salon. Salvatore kindly introduced himself to the family.

Hobbling along on a cane and wearing his fortune-telling outfit, Albert stepped up beside Flynn.

"I tried to talk to Salvatore," Albert stated woefully. "Nothing I say seems to change his mind. We need to stop him for his own good and everyone in the circus."

Before Flynn could respond, he saw a group of police officers enter the park and scatter among the crowd. His heart skipped a beat when his eyes fell upon Rena walking with one of the officers.

Her eyes found Flynn, and a big smile formed on her face. She pointed the police in Flynn's direction. An officer motioned for her to stay behind for her safety.

Salvatore, who was still talking to the family, stopped in mid-sentence when he saw all the police officers. He excused himself and darted toward Flynn. He wrapped his arm around Flynn's neck, thrusting Flynn in front of his body like a human shield. The police drew their guns and the crowd panicked, scattering in all directions.

Salvatore pulled out his pocket watch and swung it back and forth, freezing the timelines of the crowd, Rena, and the police officers. One officer had frozen in mid-run with a gun pointed at Salvatore. An eerie silence fell over the fairgrounds. No one blinked; everyone's faces were frozen in place like statues in a wax museum. Only Albert, Salvatore, Flynn, and the other circus performers were awake and unfrozen.

Salvatore's arm tightened around Flynn's neck, lifting him off the ground. Flynn's arms and legs flailed as he gasped for air. Flynn pulled on Salvatore's arm, but he couldn't loosen himself from Salvatore's grip.

"Son, don't do this," Albert pleaded. "Give yourself up. You're making things worse."

"I can make this kid disappear and erase everyone's memory," Salvatore replied in a cold tone. "I'll never give up."

"Fine," Albert retorted. "I'll take your powers away."

"No you won't!" Salvatore yelled.

Flynn's face turned blue and his windpipe felt crushed. He couldn't wriggle free.

Salvatore held up his pocket watch and swung it from side-to-side. As the watch swung faster, Albert's life timeline sped up. It was like watching a flower grow up from the ground, bud, and then blossom in time-lapse photography. Seconds turned into minutes, and hours turned into days, and then days turned into years. Albert's gray hair turned white and fell out. His wrinkles grew thick across his face and hands. His body became hunched and frail in a matter of seconds. When Salvatore stopped his watch, Albert collapsed to his knees from weakness. Flynn feared Albert might only have a few hours to live.

Using the last strength he could muster, Albert chanted barely above a whisper, "I call upon the four classical elements, wind, fire, earth, and water, to take away the powers of my son."

Rain clouds gathered in the sky, and a cold wind rustled the leaves on the trees. The tent's canvas rippled and flapped in the breeze. A bolt of lightning struck the ground a few feet from Salvatore. He jumped at the flash of lightning, but kept Flynn in his grip. The ground caught fire, and a ring surrounded Salvatore and Flynn. A gust of wind swirled around them, picking up charred dirt and twisting it into a small tornado. The wind gained strength, encircling Salvatore and Flynn and spinning them around.

Salvatore howled, "Father! What have you done?"

Flynn then saw the pocket watch slip out of Salvatore's hand. It flew through the air and landed on top of an over-turned food cart. A lightning bolt cracked from the sky and struck the watch, melting and stretching it. Like candle wax, it lost its shape and oozed down the side of the cart.

The wind subsided and raindrops fell from the sky, extinguishing the ring of fire. Salvatore and Flynn collapsed to the ground. Feeling dizzy, Flynn watched the crowd awaken from their frozen state and run out of the park.

Sammy picked up the hose from the helium tank, opened the valve, and stuck the end of it in his mouth. His body expanded like a hot air balloon, lifted off the ground, and floated away. Buster grabbed the hose and followed his brother's lead.

As Buster ascended into the evening sky, he said in a high-pitched helium voice, "Adios, amigo!"

Buster waved good-bye and smiled at Flynn. Flynn tried to wave, but his arms were too sore. Then he heard the sound of growling lions, so he looked toward the main tent.

Jack's three white rabbits had transformed into lions and stood guard in front of their master. Looking over his shoulder for an escape route, Jack slowly stepped backward. He spotted the dense forest behind the main tent.

With a gun drawn, an officer blocked Jack's path, but a lion lunged toward the officer, knocking his gun away and forcing him to retreat.

A police car tore up mud as it raced into the center of the park. The car stopped and an officer jumped out, toting a dart gun. Taking cover behind the driver's side door, the policeman aimed and fired a tranquilizer dart into the lion's hind end. The lion wobbled a few steps before rolling to the ground. The officer stepped away from the car to get a better aim. Using the scope of the gun, he found another lion in his crosshairs. He shot the second lion in the shoulder, and it dropped to the ground.

Crouching low, the lioness scratched the ground with her claws. She ran and leaped into the air. Frantically, the officer loaded another dart into the gun and pulled the trigger just as the lioness landed on top of him, pinning him to the ground. He raised his hands to protect his face. Her teeth clamped onto his forearm, cutting through his uniform and skin. The tranquilizer kicked in then, and her heavy body collapsed onto the man's chest. Two policemen ran over and rolled the lioness off the fallen officer.

Without his protection, Jack panicked and sprinted toward the forest. A couple deputies gave chase and tackled him before he got away. They handcuffed Jack and dragged him to a patrol car.

Flynn overheard shouting so he glanced back at the main tent. He saw Marcel grabbing any object he could find. Using them as weights, Marcel's muscles and body grew into that of a giant. Marcel charged past the confused officers and raced toward the forest. He picked up food carts and threw them over his shoulder. Flynn felt the ground vibrate as the carts crashed and rolled past him. The chaos slowed the officers down, allowing Marcel to escape into the forest.

Flynn heard a groaning sound, and he looked over at Salvatore. A detective approached him with handcuffs in one hand and a gun in the other. Salvatore didn't put up a fight as the officer hoisted him off the ground, cuffed him, and escorted him to a police car. Flynn picked himself off the ground and walked over to the detective. She made a radio call for two ambulances. Salvatore looked defeated as he stared at the melted watch on the food cart.

The officers arrested the remaining circus employees and put them into a police bus. Wrapped in a blanket, Cordelia sobbed as the police put her into a parked car.

Flynn felt an overwhelming sense of sadness. He didn't want Cordelia to get into trouble and felt guilty that as a result of his actions, innocent circus workers were losing their jobs and being sent to jail.

Flynn looked around and saw Albert lying on the ground. He ran over to him. He was mumbling something so Flynn crouched down to hear him better.

"Flynn, listen to me carefully," Albert said faintly. Flynn had to strain his ears to hear him. "Cordelia will die if she doesn't get to…"

Albert clutched his chest and wheezed.

"Relax. Don't strain yourself," Flynn pleaded. "The ambulance is almost here. They'll take you to the hospital, and you're going be OK."

Between heavy gasps for air, Albert said, "I'm dying, Flynn. I don't have much time…Cordelia can't live without water…She turns into a mermaid at night…She can't swim if she goes to jail…" Albert struggled to form words. "You're on your own…Please get her to water."

Overwhelmed by the moment, but aware Albert needed reassurance, Flynn said, "OK, I will."

"Promise?" Albert muttered only half conscious.

"I promise," Flynn assured him.

Two ambulances pulled up. Paramedics jumped out and ran to the back of the truck. They grabbed first-aid bags and a stretcher, rolling it over to Albert.

"Sir, are you having trouble breathing?" the paramedic asked. "Are you having arm and chest pains?"

Barely audible, Albert gasped, "Yes."

The paramedic looked at Flynn and asked, "Is he is on any heart medication?"

"Not to my knowledge, but I think he's taking medication for Alzheimer's," Flynn replied.

One paramedic checked Albert's pulse, while the other opened Albert's mouth to see if anything was blocking his breathing.

"Does your body hurt? Do you have any injuries?" the paramedic asked, shining a light into Albert's pupil.

"No," Albert managed to whisper.

The paramedic placed an oxygen mask over Albert's mouth. They carefully lifted him onto the stretcher, loaded him into the ambulance, and raced him to the hospital with lights flashing and sirens blaring.

A detective walked over to Flynn and reported, "Your parents will be here in a minute. Are you all right? Did you get hurt?"

"No, I'm OK," Flynn responded. He noticed her badge had the name Cassatt. "But you need to get Cordelia to water."

"Which one is Cordelia?" Detective Cassatt inquired.

"The girl with red hair. She turns into a mermaid after sunset," Flynn replied. "She needs water to live."

With a look of disbelief, the detective asked, "She's a real mermaid? Um, OK, we'll take good care of her. Strange things happened here tonight. Not sure how that guy turned rabbits into lions. The clowns flew away, and I've never seen a giant before. I've a lot questions that need to be answered. We'll need you to come down to the police station for questioning later tonight. But first we'll need to interrogate the circus employees. Your parents can bring you to the station when we're ready for you."

Flynn knew his story was unbelievable and that the detective wouldn't take him seriously, so he bargained. "I'll only go to the police station if you get Cordelia to water right now."

The detective held up her hand, walked away, and said dismissively, "We'll take care of it. Don't worry."

Rena watched all of this while standing behind a police car. She felt like she was in a dream. When it finally dawned on her it was real, she approached Flynn.

Flynn felt a gentle tap on his shoulder and turned around to see Rena.

"Thanks for getting me out of this mess." Flynn smiled.

"You owe me one," Rena said with a wink. Relief washed over them like a wave.

"No problem. How can I make it up to you?"

"I don't know. Maybe you can draw a picture for me?" Rena asked.

"Sure." He grinned. "I can do that."

He talked naturally with her. It felt comfortable and easy, like an inner force was pushing him to be brave. Flynn's enthusiasm turned to frustration, however, as the thought of his actions sank in. Albert stood at the brink of death. Cordelia had gone to jail and she would die without water! Flynn realized that only he could fix things.

Noticing Flynn's worried look, Rena inquired, "What's wrong?"

"Nothing." Flynn tried to hide his concern. "This is my problem. You helped me enough."

"Well, I came this far," Rena implied with determination.

She could help me, Flynn thought, *but I don't want her to get into trouble.*

"Cordelia and Albert are going to die if I don't do something. And Salvatore took all your dad's money. Albert can get it back," Flynn explained.

"What do you want me to do?" Rena volunteered.

"I need time to think of a plan," Flynn decided.

⌒➶

"Flynn, are you OK?" Flynn turned and saw his parents running toward him, followed by Rena's parents and a man wearing a badge and gun.

Georgia gave him a big hug and Ray placed his hand on his son's shoulder. Mrs. Gainsborough had tears in her eyes as she embraced her daughter. After a moment of silence, the man with a badge approached the families. Flynn noticed that his nametag read *Detective Winslow*.

Looking at Ray, Winslow stated, "Flynn can't go home tonight because we need to ask him a few questions about the circus and what happened to him. I reserved some rooms at the Grand River Motel. Get some supper and we'll call you when we're ready to interview Flynn."

Detective Winslow looked at Mrs. Gainsborough and said, "I have a room for you too, just in case we need to talk to Rena. If all goes well, everyone can leave in the morning."

Arguing won't get us anywhere Flynn thought as he looked at Rena. He shrugged his shoulders and instructed, "We'll talk later."

Rena nodded; she could sense the wheels turning inside Flynn's head.

Rena looked around and asked her dad, "Where's Deana?"

"Staying with your grandparents," Mr. Gainsborough replied.

"Come on Flynn." Ray interrupted the moment. "Let's get something to eat."

"OK," Flynn said with resignation.

⤙◯

Ray raised his voice inside the family car. "Do you know how much stress you put us through? We went to the police; we questioned neighbors, the principal, and your friends. We looked everywhere for you."

"We were worried sick," Georgia added.

"What do you have to say for yourself?" Ray asked.

"I'm sorry," Flynn apologized.

"We took time off work to look for you," Ray said, taking out his frustration on Flynn. "I might not even have a job when I get back."

"That's not Flynn's fault!" Georgia interjected. "They aren't going to fire you because you took time off work to look for Flynn. You might not have a job because your boss has no money to pay anyone! Don't blame that on Flynn."

What? My dad might lose his job? Flynn thought.

"No, Flynn didn't get me fired," Ray explained. "But I'm under a lot of pressure, and Flynn has made it worse with this little stunt. I might have a heart attack."

"He wouldn't have run away if you had just listened to him," Georgia countered.

Flynn tuned out his parents' argument. A question repeated over and over in Flynn's mind. *How I am going to save Cordelia and Albert and find Mr. Gainsborough's money so my dad won't lose his job?*

Flynn couldn't even begin to explain all the situations he faced alone. He had almost drowned, was nearly eaten by lions, was beaten-up by Marcel, and had been shot out of a cannon twice. Flynn silently stared out the car window as the argument continued in the front seat.

15

Wednesday night…

The police had reserved two rooms right next to each other on the second floor of the Grand River Motel. After checking in, Ray and Mr. Gainsborough drove off to find some fast food.

"I guess we can wait in our rooms until our husbands get back" Mrs. Gainsborough suggested.

"Sure. Flynn needs take a shower," Georgia said as she ran her fingers through Flynn's hair.

"Rena, I brought you some clothes to change into," Rena's mom added.

Flynn carried Rena's backpack of clothes as they climbed the stairs to the second floor. There was an awkward silence as they each walked to their rooms.

"I'll knock on your door when they get back," Georgia said to Mrs. Gainsborough. "I don't think they'll be long. Hopefully the police will call and this whole mess will be over soon."

"I hope so," Mrs. Gainsborough replied.

They swiped their key cards and entered their rooms.

Flynn jumped into the shower. The hot water cascaded over his face and relaxed his muscles. The physical tension of the last few days melted away. His mind was spinning. He wondered how he was going to sneak away with Rena while their parents were hanging around. He realized that any plan would require his magic pencil, but where could he find paper?

After a quick shower, he dried off and dressed. When he opened the bathroom door, he saw his mom sitting on the bed, biting her nails and watching TV.

"Feel better?" Georgia asked, tucking her hands under her legs.

"A lot." Flynn cracked a brief smile. "Do you think it would be OK if Rena and I sat in the lobby and drew some pictures while we wait for Dad?"

"Flynn, it's late." Georgia sighed.

"Pleeeease." Flynn gave her the puppy dog eyes. He still didn't have a plan, but if he could sneak away with Rena, they might figure this out together. "I'm really stressed out and drawing helps me relax."

"Okaaay," Georgia reluctantly agreed. "But I'll be down in a minute to check on you two. I want to call your grandparents and tell them you're all right. If you need paper to draw on, there are big paper liners covering the bottoms of the desk and dresser drawers."

"Thanks, Mom." Flynn gave her a hug.

Flynn opened dresser and desk drawers and found a large sheet of paper in the bottom of each drawer.

Georgia shook her head and rolled her eyes.

"I've heard of people taking motel towels but not paper liner," Georgia joked.

Flynn smiled as he left the room. He stepped sideways and knocked on the adjacent door. Rena's mom answered.

"Hi, Mrs. Gainsborough." Flynn addressed her with newfound courage. "Would it be OK if Rena and I drew some pictures while we wait for dinner? There are some tables down in the lobby. My mom said it would be OK."

"I don't see why not," Rena's mom said. "I think she's almost dressed. Come in."

"Thanks," Flynn replied, surprised by her willingness to let Rena out of the room. Flynn took a seat in the only chair. Rena's mom sat on the edge of the bed and looked at him.

"So, there's the homecoming dance in a few weeks," she remarked, a smirk on her face. "Have you thought about asking anyone?"

"Umm," Flynn answered the curve ball question. "I have someone in mind, but I'm not sure if she would say yes."

"Oh, I think you'd be surprised." She winked at him.

The bathroom door opened and Rena walked out in her everyday clothes.

"Flynn!" Rena stepped back for a moment, surprised to see him in her room. "What are you guys talking about?"

"Flynn wanted to draw in the lobby while we waited." Mrs. Gainsborough spoke for Flynn.

Rena nodded, trying to go along with Flynn's plan. She felt stressed out about going behind her mom's back, but at the same time she felt compelled to help Flynn. Deep down she cared about him.

"My mom will be down in the lobby in a few minutes. She needed to make a phone call first," Flynn reassured Mrs. Gainsborough.

"Me too. I need to call Deana and let her know what's going on."

Rena grabbed her backpack, and they stepped into the hall. She struggled to keep up with Flynn as he led her behind the motel instead of going to the lobby.

The pool was closed for the season, but there were a few lawn chairs and table next to it. Through the clump of trees behind the motel, Flynn noticed the sun setting on the horizon. Time was running out. He felt like Dorothy in *The Wizard of Oz* watching the sand flow through the hourglass.

Flynn sat down in a chair, took out his magic pencil, and unrolled the paper liners onto the table. His hand whizzed back and forth as he drew two flashlights and walkie-talkies. Using his imagination, the drawings quickly turned into real objects.

Rena watched with her mouth slightly open in amazement. She couldn't believe her eyes. She wished she had a special talent too.

"I have a plan," Flynn muttered. "Sort of."

Flynn handed her a flashlight and walkie-talkie. He placed the other two paper liners into Rena's backpack and slung it over his shoulders. Flynn wasn't sure where or how far away the hospital and jail were from the motel. Finding them on foot was an option, but it would take too long, or they might get lost. They needed to be careful too, because the police and their parents would soon be cruising around looking for them.

Suddenly, the branches of a nearby tree rustled and crackled. Startled by the sound, Flynn and Rena looked up at the trees behind the pool. They shined their flashlights on the trees and saw Sammy and Buster floating in the air. They were using the branches to hold themselves still in the wind.

Rena looked at Flynn and uttered, "Wow, this is so surreal."

Flynn yelled to Buster, "How did you find me?"

Buster smiled and said in a squeaky helium voice, "I followed your parents' car."

"What are you doing here?" Flynn asked.

"We're here to help," Buster explained. "I don't care about Salvatore, but Albert always treated us well. What can we do?"

"We need to save Cordelia too," Flynn said, relieved for the extra help. "She needs water soon or she'll die. I promised Albert I would save her. I have a plan, but we need to find Marcel. Do you think he will help too?"

Buster nodded. "Yeah, he'll help because he likes Cordelia. Sammy knows just where to find him. Grab onto my feet. Sammy will carry your friend."

Buster swung his feet close the ground.

Flynn looked at Rena with uncertainty. He'd never been a fan of heights, especially after being shot out of a cannon. But they both knew this was the quickest way to get to the jail and to the hospital. Flying in the sky without a parachute was extremely dangerous, and Flynn wanted to make sure Rena was ready for the challenge.

"Will you take a risk with me?" Flynn asked Rena. His heart wanted her to say yes.

For the first time, she felt nervous around Flynn. It was almost as if their roles had been reversed. She looked up at the clowns, and then back at Flynn.

"I thought you would never ask," Rena said, smiling.

Flynn latched onto Buster's leg. Buster let go of the branch and floated away. Rena reached up and grabbed on to Sammy's ankles and he released his grip. Like hot air balloons, they rose above the trees until they saw rooftops, tiny specks of car headlights, and streetlamps dangling below their feet. Flynn looked in amazement at the network of streets and buildings that made up the city below. A full moon slowly appeared, illuminating the cloudless sky, and a favorable breeze blew them across town.

"Look!" Flynn said and tugged on Buster's foot. "I see the hospital!" At this height it was very quiet and peaceful. They could see the layout of the entire city. Flynn hardly had to raise his voice for Buster to hear him.

"Yeah, I see it," Buster replied. "Remember where it's located so we can find it later."

Flynn made a mental note of the location.

"And over there is the police station and jail," Buster indicated to two buildings. "It's on the north side of town near the forest."

"Where are we going?" Flynn questioned.

"Marcel is hiding in a forest, just outside of town," Buster said.

They floated to the outskirts of the city, watching intently as the national forest came into focus.

Sammy and Buster opened their mouths and slowly let the helium expel from their lungs. They descended gently on to a grassy hill. Flynn and Rena dropped softly to the ground as Sammy and Buster's bodies deflated back to their normal size and weight.

Buster waved his hand and requested, "Follow me."

Flynn and Rena turned on their flashlights as Buster led them along the hiking trail. The sounds of crickets chirping, owls hooting, and coyotes howling filled the cool night air. After several minutes, they reached the lake they had seen earlier from above.

"Are you sure he's here?" Flynn asked, a hint of skepticism in his voice.

"Over there," Buster said, pointing straight ahead.

Rena and Flynn shined the flashlights to a steep hill behind the lake. When they approached, Flynn saw a cave cut into the hillside.

"You first," Sammy said to Flynn cautiously.

Flynn swung the flashlight back and forth as he entered the cave. The cave's walls and ceiling glistened with moisture. Rena felt the air temperature drop about ten degrees, which gave her goose bumps. Flynn's beam of light fell upon a pack of rats feasting on a pile of rotten dead fish. Rena gagged on the awful smell. Startled by the presence of humans, the rats scattered in panic. Disgusted and unsettled, everyone clung to the cave walls as the rats ran out the mouth of the cave; the rat's fur and tails brushed against everyone's legs. Rena let out a stifled scream.

A voice echoed through the cave. "Who's there?"

Buster recognized Marcel's voice and shouted, "It's Sammy and Buster."

Walking deeper into the cave, Flynn smelled smoke, and he saw the glow of a campfire surrounded by rocks. Marcel was sitting with his back against the cave wall.

Still astonished by Marcel's size, Rena gasped. "Holy cow! He's huge!"

"What's Flynn doing here?" Marcel boiled with anger.

Marcel jumped to his feet and bumped his head against the cave ceiling. He bent down and rubbed his head.

"I knew you lied to me!" Marcel clinched his fists and shouted. "You said you didn't tell anyone you were kidnapped."

Rena flinched and grabbed Flynn's arm.

"I came here for your help," Flynn implored calmly.

"Help? Why should I help you?" Marcel fired back. "I'm a fugitive from the law because of you."

"Cordelia is locked in jail," Flynn continued. He knew this would make Marcel at least hear him out. "I told the police she needs water to survive, but they didn't believe me. They're not going to do anything. I know you don't like me, but Cordelia and Albert need you."

Marcel looked at Sammy and Buster. "Is that true?"

They both nodded, and Marcel ran his giant hand through his hair as he took a deep breath.

"OK," Marcel said with some hesitation. "I'll help you. So what is the game plan?"

Flynn suggested, "Well, I thought we could split up into two groups. Each group will get a walkie-talkie so we can stay in contact. Buster, Marcel, and I will go to the jail and break Cordelia out. Rena and Sammy will find what room Albert is staying in at the hospital. We'll call you on the walkie-talkie after we rescue Cordelia. Then you can tell us which room they're holding Albert in."

"Sounds kind of risky." Marcel raised his eyebrows. "Why should I risk my neck for you?"

"Marcel, here is your chance to be a knight in shining armor." Buster teased. "You can rescue Cordelia. I've seen the way you look at her... Everyone knows you like her."

Marcel pouted and said, "Shut up, Buster!"

Buster fluttered his eyelashes, puckered his lips, and teased in a high pitched tone, "Oh, Marcel, thanks for saving me! Come here so I can give you a hug. Smoochie, smoochie."

Marcel grabbed Buster by the shirt and lifted him off the ground. Buster threw his hands up in surrender.

"I'm just joking," Buster repeated over and over again.

"You say one more word about Cordelia," Marcel warned him, "and I'm going to pound you into the ground!"

Marcel dropped Buster.

Buster immediately backpedaled and apologized, "I'm sorry. Just kidding. Relax, take it easy."

Sammy calmed things down by saying, "Easy, you two. We're on the same side."

"Flynn, what about the police?" Sammy asked. "They're not going to sit back and let you take Cordelia without a fight."

"Sammy, you're right," Flynn acknowledged. "Does anyone have any better ideas?"

Everyone sensed the urgency, but no safe plan emerged. Flynn had no choice; he had to take the lead.

"Maybe Buster could distract the police while we rescue Cordelia," Flynn suggested.

Sammy looked unconvinced and waited for more details.

Buster looked at Flynn and said with reassurance, "I'm a clown. I know how to draw attention. I'm always figuring out things as I go along."

"I'll see you guys in twenty years after you get out of prison," Sammy said nervously.

"If anyone wants to back out, now is the time," Flynn offered. "But realistically, we need everyone. Albert and Cordelia need everyone. Who's coming with me?"

After a few moments of consideration, everyone agreed to the plan. Flynn had assembled a team. They were ready to follow him into danger.

Marcel extinguished the fire with dirt and led them out of the cave and back into the forest.

As they emerged from the forest, they split up into two groups. Sammy and Rena headed toward the hospital, and Buster and Marcel followed Flynn to the jail. On the surface, everything seemed under control. Flynn had a plan and a willing team, but the night would soon turn into chaos.

16

~

The police station was on the north side of town, not far from the forest. It consisted of two buildings—a large jail for the criminals, and a smaller building with offices and police officers.

The small building had a well-kept lawn and parking lot with several police cars. The entrance and front sidewalk had a covered roof held up with steel pillars.

The jail had concrete block walls, and steel bars covered the windows. Fewer than half of the windows were lit. Spotlights were bright as day within the courtyard. A chain link fence surrounded the perimeter with barbed wire spiraling around the top.

Marcel, Buster, and Flynn stood behind some trees and bushes a few yards away from the fence. Cautiously, they watched for the guards, but they didn't see any movement. They needed to move quickly or else risk being caught. Being captured was one danger, being shot was another.

Marcel looked down at Flynn and asked, "What's the game plan?"

"You're going to punch a hole through the concrete wall. When the alarm rings, the police will run out of their offices. Buster, can you stall the police while Marcel grabs Cordelia?"

Buster nodded and ran to the end of the covered walkway near the office building, keeping out of sight. He grabbed the first support column and then stretched around the opposite column. He continued to weave in, out, and around the columns, creating a spider-web barrier. His body, legs, and arms were stretched so thin that Flynn could barely see the web.

Flynn sat down on the ground and pulled out his pencil and paper liner from Rena's backpack. He laid the paper on the ground and drew the exterior wall of the concrete building.

"What are you doing?" Marcel asked anxiously. "We don't have time for you to draw pictures."

"You'll see," Flynn responded, not allowing Marcel to bully him.

After completing the sketch, he said, "When you break through the concrete wall, make sure the hole is no bigger than my drawing."

Marcel held his fist up to the paper; both were roughly the same size.

"Are you ready?" Flynn asked.

"Yeah, I guess so," Marcel responded. "How do we know which cell Cordelia is in?

"Jump over the fence and lift me up so I can look through the windows," Flynn instructed.

Marcel sprinted toward the fence and leaped over it. Flynn followed him to the fence and climbed up half way.

Marcel reached back over the fence, wrapped his giant hand around Flynn's waist, and raised him up and over the barbed wire. Then, he ran to the building and lifted Flynn to the nearest window so he could look inside.

Flynn shook his head and pointed to another window. Marcel stepped to the next one and Flynn shook his head again. When he peered into the third window, he saw Cordelia lying on a wooden bench. The police officers had placed her in a holding cell until she was ready for questioning. Salvatore was soaking a stack of paper towels underneath a drinking fountain. He carried the towels over to Cordelia and gently placed them over her legs, trying to keep them as moist as possible. Her legs tried to fuse together, but it didn't work.

"I found her!" Flynn exclaimed in an urgent whisper. He felt discouraged because he never wanted to see Salvatore again.

Marcel set Flynn on the ground and cocked his fist like a boxer. *BAM!* His fist blasted through the wall like a cannon ball. Chunks of concrete exploded in all directions. He pulled his fist back, clearing away the rubble and leaving a hole large enough for Cordelia to climb through.

When the dust finally settled, Flynn peered inside. He heard the screeching alarm bouncing off the concrete walls. He saw Salvatore covered in dust and holding onto his ears. After the initial shock wore off, Salvatore's face turned to rage.

"This is all your fault!" Salvatore yelled at Flynn.

"Bring Cordelia to Marcel!" Flynn commanded, keeping his emotions in check. "We're taking her to water!"

An officer ran toward the holding room door and fumbled with his keys.

Without wasting any more time, Salvatore cradled Cordelia in his arms and carried her to the wall. Marcel stuck his hand through the hole, and Salvatore placed Cordelia on Marcel's palm. He gently pulled Cordelia through the hole.

"My turn," Salvatore said, seizing his opportunity for escape. Salvatore began to crawl out of the hole, but Marcel pushed him back inside. Salvatore tumbled to the floor of the holding cell.

Flynn quickly covered the hole with his drawing. Within a matter of seconds, new concrete blocks suddenly appeared. Flynn's drawing repaired the prison wall and trapped Salvatore inside! He heard Salvatore pounding his fist against the wall and yelling, "Noooooo!"

The sound satisfied Flynn, but he had no time to enjoy it. He stuffed the last piece of paper, the walkie-talkie, and the flashlight into the backpack and slung it over his shoulder.

Marcel kneeled down on the ground and Flynn climbed onto his shoulders like a parrot. When Flynn had a firm grip, Marcel stood up and held Cordelia close to his heart with one hand. He broke into a full run and leaped over the chain link fence.

"Head west toward the hospital!" Flynn shouted.

Flynn glanced back at the police station. He saw several police officers run out of the office building and straight into Buster's web. The farther the officers ran, the farther Buster's body stretched until they could run no further. Like rocks flying out of a slingshot, the officers shot backward and tumbled to the ground.

Buster unwrapped himself from the columns, and his body went back to its normal size. He ran to catch up with Flynn and Marcel, but more officers emerged from the office building and tackled Buster. Flynn watched in horror as the officers handcuffed him.

"Oh no!" Flynn shouted to Marcel. "Buster is caught!"

"What?" Marcel yelled.

Things then went from bad to worse. Another group of police officers sprinted to their parked cars.

"Now they're coming after us!" Flynn exclaimed with adrenaline pumping through his veins.

With flashing lights, blaring sirens, and squealing tires, the police raced out of the parking lot.

"We need to go back for Buster," Flynn protested. "He's in trouble."

"No, we don't have time," Marcel yelled back, without breaking his stride.

"We can't just leave him there. They'll arrest him and put him in jail with Salvatore."

"That was the risk he was willing to take," Marcel responded angrily and refused to turn around.

For a moment, Flynn wondered if he should jump off Marcel's shoulder and go back to help, but he knew he couldn't take on a squad of police officers alone. He felt sick to his stomach as the officers dragged Buster toward the station.

Out of nowhere, two large bird-like creatures appeared in the dark sky. Like eagles chasing their prey, they swooped toward the police officers and smashed into their backs, causing them to drop like bowling pins. The officers released their grip on Buster.

"Rego! Paula!" Flynn cried out. "Salvatore didn't erase Paula's memory!"

Buster looked at the fallen officers with a grin and then into the night sky, searching for his lifesavers. Rego and Paula circled back into view. They swooped down and scooped Buster off the sidewalk, flying him toward the forest.

"Wa-hoo!" Flynn cheered from atop Marcel's shoulders, pumping his fist in the air.

"What happened?" Marcel asked without looking back.

"Rego and Paula came back! They saved Buster!" Flynn exclaimed.

"Good," Marcel grunted as he barreled down the middle of the street. Flynn ducked and dodged as street lamps flew over his head. He gripped Marcel's shoulder tighter as oncoming cars swerved and honked, trying to avoid Marcel's massive body. One car drove off the road and hit a parked car. Steam rolled out the sides of the crumpled hood.

Flynn had a bad feeling about Marcel's bold actions and recklessness.

"Marcel, maybe we should—" Flynn started to say.

His sentence trailed off when they turned a corner and saw a police roadblock at the next intersection. Flynn looked over his shoulder and saw two more police cars chasing behind them.

"We're trapped!" Flynn shouted, and his heart sunk.

The police drew their guns.

"Stop or we'll shoot!" an officer screeched through a bullhorn. "I repeat, stop or we'll open fire!"

"Marcel, stop!" Flynn yelped, but Marcel didn't slow down.

Flynn panicked and climbed around Marcel's back like he was on a piggyback ride. Just as they passed a group of parked cars, Marcel ripped off a car hood and held it up like a shield. The officers fired their guns, and Flynn heard the sound of bullets slamming against the metal.

"Are you crazy?" Flynn yelled.

"Just hold on and shut up," Marcel roared back, still holding Cordelia with one arm and the car hood in the other.

Flynn peeked over Marcel's shoulder and gasped when he saw the police barricade.

"Hold on tight," Marcel warned.

With a loud growl, he leaped over the police roadblock. Flynn looked down at the policemen. They didn't fire any more bullets, and instead they just watched in awe as the giant man with a woman in his arms and a teenager on his back sailed through the air. Marcel's landing was a little rough, and Flynn's neck felt whiplashed, but they were free and clear. Or so they thought.

"*Wa-hoo!*" Flynn yelled. "Way to go!"

Flynn glimpsed a smile on Marcel's face, but Marcel stayed silent as he barreled ahead.

"I think we're clear!" Flynn yelled, but seconds later sirens filled the air again. Flynn glanced back and saw more police cars headed their way.

"Uh-oh," Flynn uttered.

"You really thought they'd give up that easily?" Marcel asked, breathing heavily.

Flynn stayed quiet and readjusted his grip. He peered over Marcel's shoulder and saw a sign with a big red cross on the side of a building a half mile ahead.

"I see the hospital straight ahead," Flynn said into Marcel's ear.

"Me too," Marcel responded.

Flynn heard the sirens grow louder as Marcel desperately tried to outrun them. With the end in sight, Marcel increased his speed, creating a huge gap between them and the cops.

Flynn reached into the backpack, grabbed the walkie-talkie, and spoke into the receiver, "Rena, what room is Albert in?"

Flynn heard a crackling noise but no response. Flynn was worried. *Maybe they got caught by the police.* He repeated his call. After a moment of static, Flynn heard Rena's faint voice on the walkie-talkie.

"We're on the second floor, Room 202, facing Main Street. Hold on, I'll signal with the flashlight."

Rena felt relieved to hear Flynn's voice. Albert was getting weaker by the minute and there wasn't anything she could do to help him. Standing by an open window, she waved the flashlight, hoping Flynn saw her signal.

⌒᧐

As Marcel approached the hospital, Flynn's eyes scanned the hospital windows for Rena's signal. He spotted her standing in the open window. Flynn felt relief despite the dangerous situation. The police had lost track of them for the moment.

Flynn pointed to her. "Up there, on the second floor."

"Yep," Marcel said, panting. "I see her."

Marcel jumped over a fence and stood in front of the hospital. He plucked Flynn off his shoulder and lifted him up to Albert's window. Flynn climbed through it, turned to Marcel, and tossed him the walkie-talkie.

"We'll meet you back in the forest by the lake," he instructed. "We'll call you if we need any help."

"I'll take care of the police by leading them on a wild goose chase," Marcel replied. "But Cordelia will be safer with you."

Flynn extended his arms and said, "OK, hand me Cordelia."

Cordelia was motionless in the palm of Marcel's hand. He passed her to Flynn and disappeared into the night. Flynn struggled to hold onto to her, so Sammy came over to help.

Glancing out the window, Flynn watched Marcel lead the police away from the hospital. Now focusing his attention on the room, Flynn saw Rena standing next to the Albert, who was lying motionless in the hospital bed. He had aged even more. An oxygen mask had been placed over his mouth, and a heart monitor beeped slowly in the background.

Sammy helped Flynn put Cordelia on the bed next to Albert.

A TV hung on the back wall of the room. The volume was turned down low, but Flynn heard the news anchor say, "Breaking news, we have a police chase in downtown Grand River. They appear to be chasing, and this may sound crazy, a giant!"

Flynn blocked out the television and focused on his next move. *What can I do about this?* Flynn thought. *I'm an artist, not a doctor.*

Sammy insisted in a hushed tone, "Now what?

Cordelia's leg twitched and her eyes fluttered open. Without raising her head from the pillow, she mumbled words that made no sense. Flynn moved closer to the bed and bent down to listen to her. When her eyes finally focused, she scowled at Flynn.

She turned her head away and growled, "What do you want? Haven't you done enough damage?"

"Damage?" Flynn hadn't expected this response. "Your grandfather asked me to help."

Cordelia then looked at Flynn and their eyes connected. Her face turned red with anger.

"Help?" Cordelia snapped in a weak but determined voice. "You call this help? The circus is gone. My dad is in jail. My grandfather is dying. And I am sick. You've helped my family enough."

Flynn dropped his head. "I didn't mean to hurt you or your family."

She rolled over and buried her face in her grandfather's chest.

Flynn could barely hear Cordelia's words.

"If I can't swim, then let me spend the rest of my life with the only family I have left. Just leave me alone," she said in a weak voice.

Her tears dampened Albert's hospital gown.

Flynn felt helpless and hopeless. He didn't know what to say, and he couldn't think of any more options. His eyes searched the room for clues on how to resolve things. Without panic, he closed his eyes and let his subconscious run like paint on a canvas. His memories filled the blank white space with images from the past few days. Cordelia's tarnished locket popped into his painting. Flynn's imagination saw the locket open. Inside, there was a picture of Albert as a young man. Like a splash of cold water, Flynn snapped back to reality. He knew what to do.

Cordelia looked pale and soon fainted from lack of water. Flynn saw the locket hanging around her neck, so he opened it. Then he gently lifted the locket over her flowing red hair. He pulled out the pencil and paper from the backpack, sat on the hospital room floor, and leaned against the cold metal frame of the hospital bed. He placed the open locket at the top of the paper and concentrated on the photograph. He studied every feature of Albert's younger face and summoned all of his creative skills.

"What are you doing?" Sammy asked, a bit of confusion in his voice. "How is this going to help Albert?"

Flynn blocked out Sammy's voice as he concentrated on his drawing. All he could hear was lead gliding across the paper. His eyes darted back and forth from the locket to the drawing. His imagination traveled from his mind to his hand and out through the tip of the pencil. After adding some last-minute details, Flynn held up the drawing for Sammy and Rena.

"Looks perfect!" Rena said. "What are you going to do?"

"Just wait and see. I hope this works."

Flynn stood up and looked down at Albert's frail body. He removed the oxygen mask and placed the drawing over Albert's face. He focused all of his thoughts and energy on the image. The paper draped over Albert like a wet cloth. The contour lines of the drawing traced around his face and dissolved into the pores of his skin.

The heart monitor beeped faster and erratically. Albert's breathing sped up and his body trembled beneath the blanket. Sammy paced the floor with his arms crossed. Suddenly, Albert's breathing and heart stopped; the heart monitor flat lined, triggering an alarm. Sammy ran to the bed.

Flynn punched the wall and said, "No, don't leave us now. This has to work!"

Flynn leaned down and placed his hands on Albert's shoulders, gripping them tightly. Like a bolt of lightning, a shock ran through his hands and jolted Albert's body like a defibrillator. Flynn stumbled backward, almost falling to the floor, but Sammy caught him just in time.

Adding to the confusion, the heart monitor beeped rapidly.

"What happened?" Sammy asked. "How did you do that?

Still stunned, Flynn responded, "I don't know."

Suddenly, there was a clambering in the hall. Rena cracked the door open and looked out. The nurse was running from behind her counter with a concerned look on her face; the guard reached for his walkie-talkie, and his eyes widened with wonder at the situation. Rena stepped into the hall. On the inside her stomach was tied in a knot and her brain was torn in two directions. *Did Albert need a nurse, or would Flynn's special talent save him?* If she let the nurse and the guard into the room, they would catch everyone and who knows what would happen. It could all be over for everyone, including Cordelia. She decided to put faith in Flynn and risk the possible consequences. With outward calm, Rena stepped into the hall.

"I'm sorry, it's my fault," Rena spoke to the nurse. "Everything is OK in here. No need for panic. I was adjusting Albert's blanket, and I accidently knocked the connection for his heart monitor off his chest. I put it back on and he's fine now. I'm so sorry to have caused you concern."

Rena waited to see what the nurse and guard would do. They had stopped to process what she had said, but neither said anything. Rena couldn't breathe while she waited for them to react. She wondered if they noticed her heart pounding beneath her shirt.

"OK." The nurse seemed to relax. "Let us know if he needs anything."

"I will," Rena replied.

The nurse and the guard returned to the nurse's desk, muttering to each other. Rena quickly went back inside Albert's room.

Rena, Flynn, and Sammy watched in awe as the wrinkles on Albert's skin melted away and his hair thickened. Starting from the roots, his hair changed from gray to light brown. His age clock reversed until his cheeks turned a rosy pink. Youthfulness radiated from Albert's head down to his toes. He looked like the photograph when he was forty years old.

Everyone was speechless, letting out a sigh of relief.

"How did your drawing make Albert younger?" Sammy asked.

"Albert gave me a special talent: the ability to turn my drawings into reality through the power of my imagination," Flynn answered, beaming with confidence.

"Wow!" Rena exclaimed. "That's awesome!"

The steady beeping of the heart monitor dominated the room. Albert raised his hand and pulled off the blankets. He lifted his head and smiled at everyone. His smile slowly disappeared, however, when he saw Cordelia's frail body.

"She needs water!" Albert exclaimed as he jumped out of bed.

17

~

"**H**er skin is dry." Albert said with concern.

"Flynn, draw a tub of water," Rena urged.

Flynn looked inside the backpack and said, "I don't have any more paper. I need a canvas big enough to draw a full-size tub."

"What about the floor? That's a big enough," Albert piped up.

"Good idea!" Flynn declared.

He sat down on the floor and started to draw a sunken tub. But as Flynn pressed the pencil against the hard ceramic tile, the lead snapped, leaving only a wood stub.

"Darn it!" Flynn exclaimed. "Where are we going to find a pencil sharpener?"

"Let's try something else," Albert said in a rush.

To keep Cordelia moist, they poured pitchers of water over her legs, but it wasn't enough to fuse them together. Since that wasn't working, Rena came up with another idea. She grabbed a blanket from the bed and stuck it underneath the faucet in the bathroom. She draped the water-soaked blanket over Cordelia's legs.

"That should help for now," Albert said. "But we need to get her out of here fast."

Flynn rolled a wheelchair over to the hospital bed, and with Sammy's help, lifted Cordelia into the chair.

"There's a lake in the forest close by," Flynn informed Albert.

"What about the officer outside the room?" Sammy asked cautiously. "We need to distract him before we can escape."

"How?" Flynn asked.

"If we switch the walkie-talkie to the police frequency," Sammy suggested, "maybe we can call in a false report."

"We'll say that Marcel is on a rampage in the streets and all police officers are needed," Flynn said, his face lighting up. "When the officer leaves, we can make our escape."

"Good idea," Albert agreed. "Let me see the walkie-talkie."

Rena handed Albert the walkie-talkie. He changed the signal to the universal police frequency.

Flynn opened the door just enough to see down the hallway. The officer was leaning against the reception counter as he talked to a pretty young nurse.

Pressing the power button, Albert said in an official-sounding voice, "Calling all officers in the vicinity of General Hospital. We have a disturbance. We have a large, muscular, unidentified man who needs to be disarmed, detained, and taken in for questioning. All officers report immediately to the parking lot for further orders."

Albert let go of the button and looked at the others.

"Did that sound believable?" he asked.

Flynn nodded, opened the door a sliver, and peered down the hall. The officer lowered the walkie-talkie from his ear, clipped it to his belt, and ran left to the nearest elevator, in the opposite direction of Albert's room.

Albert grabbed his clothes from the dresser next to the bed. He changed into his pants, shirt, shoes, and fortune-teller robe.

Flynn pushed the wheelchair to the door, then looked out and said, "Come on, let's go! The guard is gone."

"Wait!" Sammy stopped them. "If we walk past the nurse, she may suspect something and call security. We should go in the opposite direction. There should be elevators that way too."

"Good idea," Flynn said and pushed the wheelchair into the hallway. "We'll go to the right."

The nurse had her head buried in paperwork behind a tall counter. Visiting hours were over, so the hall was empty. After a few twists and turns through the hallway, they saw signs to the elevators in the north wing. This was perfect, as the main entrance faced south and the forest was to the north.

Stepping into the elevator, Albert pushed the first floor button. Nervously, they watched as the elevator's lighted numbers counted down. When the elevator stopped and the doors opened, Flynn cautiously stuck his head out, looking left and right. A police officer stood in the lobby facing the north exit. Flynn pulled his head back inside the elevator.

"A cop is guarding the exit," he reported. "Now what are we going to do?"

He looked at them for help, but they shrugged their shoulders. Flynn paused for a moment and then responded, "Maybe we can pull the rug out from underneath him."

Sammy looked puzzled. "I don't follow you."

Flynn explained his idea. Sammy smiled and nodded in agreement.

Rena held the elevator door open as Sammy crouched down, and flattened out his body like a carpet. Once flat, Sammy curled his body into a carpet roll. Flynn pushed Sammy down the hall, unrolling his body toward the exit. Sammy's body stretched down the hall, his head almost touching the sliding doors. He lay quietly and still, awaiting the next move. Flynn retreated back inside the elevator.

Rena and Albert stepped into the hallway, avoiding Sammy's flattened body by walking along the right side of him. Flynn followed, pushing the wheelchair along the left side. They kept their eyes on the police officer pacing back and forth. Without warning, the officer turned around. He must have recognized Cordelia from when she was arrested in Abner Park. The officer's eyes widened, his hand moved to his gun holster, and he broke into a run. When he stepped on Sammy, however, his boots sank into Sammy's rubbery body, which slowed him down. At first, the officer's eyes narrowed in anger, but then his eyes widened as Sammy's body pulled the officer's legs out from underneath him. The officer tumbled to the floor, and before he could stand back up, Sammy wrapped his body around him like a blanket. Like a carpet roll, they rolled past Flynn. That was Flynn's cue to run, so he pushed the wheel-chair out the door with all his strength.

Sammy shook his body back into its normal size and shape. Then he gave the dizzy officer a push, sending him sprawling onto the elevator floor. Sammy hit the top floor button and slid between the elevator doors as they closed. Flynn heard the officer yell out in anger and confusion. Once outside the hospital, everyone sprinted into the night.

∽◯

The closer they got to the forest, the more rural the landscape became. There weren't any more houses and the sidewalk ultimately led them to a gravel-hiking trail. There weren't any streetlights; the only light came from the full moon.

As they entered the forest, they heard a sudden rustling of tree branches.

"Shh!" Flynn whispered, holding up his hand. "Don't move."

Everyone froze. They didn't dare breathe.

A gigantic Marcel emerged from behind a group of trees. Rena and Flynn drew a deep breath.

"Marcel! You scared us," Flynn said with both relief and exasperation.

"I can see that. I've been waiting for you guys," Marcel said impatiently.

"Sorry. We had to dodge an officer at the hospital," Flynn explained.

Marcel glanced down at Cordelia and said, "She doesn't look good."

"The lake is close. I remember how to get there," Rena declared. "Come on. Follow me."

Rena's voice was drowned out by the thundering sound of a helicopter. Everyone looked up and saw a spotlight skimming over the trees.

"Quick, hide over here!" Marcel shouted.

Marcel broke off several tree branches and stacked them into a pile. With Flynn pushing the wheel chair, everyone hunched over and hid underneath the stack of branches. Marcel didn't have any cover, so he snapped off a weeping willow tree at its base and hid underneath its umbrella of dense leaves.

When the helicopter approached, it's spotlight shined down on the weeping willow and paused. Flynn held his breath, praying that they wouldn't get caught.

18

⁓

It seemed like an eternity, but the spotlight finally moved on. The sound of the police helicopter faded away, and Flynn let out a sigh of relief.

"That was a close one," Marcel said. "They'll be back. We should keep moving."

Flynn pushed Cordelia's wheelchair through the tall grass. His arms were too tired, and his back was sore. He grunted with frustration when the wheels became stuck in the mud; he couldn't go any further.

Flynn looked up at Marcel and begged, "Can you help me?"

Without a word, Marcel picked Cordelia up and cradled her in one arm. Flynn discarded the wheelchair underneath a bush.

Storm clouds covered the moon and raindrops fell from the sky. Flynn looked up at Cordelia's limp body. He didn't see any movement under the blanket, and a cool chill ran up the arch of his neck. *What if she dies before we get to the lake?*

Armed with two flashlights, they traveled deeper into the national forest. Rena's shortcut saved time, but it was a rough path to follow. Bushes, rocks, and roots littered the trail. It twisted up hills and through valleys.

Rena pointed and informed them, "The lake should be behind those trees."

Using his free arm, Marcel cleared a path for the rest of the group.

Flynn saw the lake surrounded by a sandy beach. Not very far away, Buster sat on a fallen tree trunk while Paula and Rego paced back and forth.

"You guys made it!" Buster exclaimed when he saw everyone emerge from the forest. "We thought you were caught by the police."

"We had a few close calls, but we escaped with everyone's help," Flynn responded.

Marcel placed Cordelia down on the beach sand and Albert removed her blanket. Flynn shined the flashlight on Cordelia's body. Her pale skin had turned blue. Her eyes were closed and she was gasping for breath.

"Flynn, help me carry her to the water," Albert pleaded.

Albert placed his hands under Cordelia's knees, and Flynn gently lifted her shoulders. They waded into the lake until the water was waist high. Albert lowered Cordelia's feet into the water and released his grip while Flynn held her shoulders and head above the water.

Flynn stared at her motionless body, looking for any signs of life. Her long hair fanned out like feathers on top of the water. Raindrops cascaded along her cheeks; she looked like she was crying.

Flynn knew what he had to do. Cordelia had saved him from drowning, so he had to "drown" her to save her life. Flynn let go of her shoulders and she sank into the lake. Water washed over her face, slipped through her fingers, and consumed her hair. Her lips opened and bubbles floated out as water poured into her mouth.

Cordelia opened her eyes and squirmed in the water. Scales pushed through the skin on her feet. Her legs fused together, transformed into a fishtail, and kicked a spout of water into the air. Her lungs filled with the only fluid that satisfied her dreams, and her thirst for life sent ripples along the water's surface.

Flynn silently watched Cordelia, and for brief a moment, their eyes locked. Her eyes hypnotized Flynn, and he couldn't turn away from her beauty. Suddenly, she raised her head out of the water and scowled at him, and then she looked over at her grandfather. With a splash, she jumped to the surface of the water, wrapped her arms around Albert, and gave him a tight hug.

"I love you, Grandpa," Cordelia whispered.

"I love you too, honey." Albert beamed with pride. "I'm so happy you're OK."

"What happened?" Cordelia looked surprise. "You look so young."

"I am young, and I feel great." Albert chuckled.

"How?" Cordelia looked baffled.

"I helped Flynn develop his artistic talent. He drew the photo from your locket, and his drawing saved my life."

"Really? But what happened to Dad? Where's Dad?" Cordelia asked, looking around. "Did he escape too?"

"No," Albert replied. "He belongs in jail. He needs to face the consequences for his bad decisions."

"But you can save him!" Cordelia pleaded.

"Not this time sweetie."

She shot Flynn an angry glance. Then, without warning, she dove back into the water and swam out into the middle of the lake.

Flynn hoped Cordelia would forgive him. She lost her mom and dad, but she still had her grandfather. Flynn felt bad for her, but in his heart he knew he had done the right thing.

As they walked along the beach, Albert placed his hand on Flynn's shoulder and said, "Thanks for all your help."

"You're welcome," Flynn responded with a smile. "Thanks for helping me become a better artist. I hope Cordelia doesn't stay mad at me forever."

"Don't worry. I'll talk to her," Albert reassured him. "Deep down, she knows that her father was wrong. She was just blinded by all the money and jewelry. Ever since her mother died, Salvatore has tried to make her happy with gifts."

Flynn nodded his head, unable to respond.

"I didn't catch your name, young lady?" Albert said turning to Rena.

"My name is Rena," she replied. "Rena Gainsborough."

"I'm Albert," he introduced himself, winking at her. "I want to thank you too."

"Flynn did most of the work," Rena implied, dismissing any credit. "Flynn said you give people special powers?"

"I help people develop their natural talents," Albert said modestly. "But it only works if they appreciate their skills. What is your passion in life?"

Rena searched her soul. "That's a hard choice because I love art and music, but if I had to choose, it would be music"

"I see. Good choice," Albert said. "I was a musician myself, a long time ago. For everything you have done, let me thank you by giving you a gift."

"You don't have to do that," Rena said, feeling awkward. "What I did was minor compared to everyone else."

"Nonsense," Albert retorted. He wouldn't take no for an answer. "Let me see your hand."

Rena stuck out her left hand, her palm facing up. The clouds parted, the rain stopped, and bright moonlight flooded over everyone. The light revealed the creases in her hand, so Albert read her palm.

"Ah, yes," Albert said. "I definitely see music in your future."

Buster was close enough to listen in on their conversation. He came over with a lighter because he knew Albert's next move. Albert bent down and grabbed a few grains of beach sand. Buster flicked on his lighter.

Albert closed his eyes and chanted from memory. "I call on the four classical elements, wind, fire, earth, and water. Wind moves sand. Fire creates earth and ash. Earth absorbs water. Water quenches fire. Give Rena the ability to compose music from her imagination that will inspire people to dance."

A breeze blew the sand through the lighter's flame. The sand burst into small explosions as it turned into ash. A small spring shot up from the lake like a fountain and split in two directions. One extinguished the lighter's flame, and the other doused the charred sand. The ash fell into Rena's palm, and a shiver ran up her spine.

"Wow," Rena whispered as she took a few steps backward. Her mind filled with musical notes.

"Are you all right?" Flynn asked, concerned for his friend.

"She'll be all right," Albert reassured him. "She's overwhelmed by the moment."

"Where did you get your powers?" Flynn asked, a puzzled look on his face.

Albert smiled and sighed. "That, my boy, is a story for another time."

"What are you going to do now?" Flynn wondered. "The police will be looking for you."

"We're going to be just fine," Albert assured him. "Maybe, we'll head south to Mexico or east to Europe. Cordelia and I will start a new circus. A circus that entertains people, not steal from them. And someday, when she's ready, it'll be hers. And hopefully," he paused and turned to the others, "Buster, Sammy, Paula, Rego, and Marcel will join us."

Albert gave them a wink and then looked back at Flynn. "By the way, we're always looking for new recruits. What are your plans after high school?"

"Thanks. I appreciate the offer, but I'm going to art school, even though my dad won't be happy," Flynn said. "He wants me to learn a trade." Flynn sighed. "But I'll need to confront him someday. I guess it's now or never."

"Well, *you* need to be the one to decide what *you* want out of life," Albert said. "Find your life's purpose and don't live someone else's dreams. Create the life *you* want to lead. People will pay you for your talents as long you don't take advantage of them."

Flynn saw Albert as a grandfather figure, eager to guide him along life's journey.

"Thanks for the advice, and for caring," Flynn said.

Albert rested his hand on Flynn's shoulder. "Having been a circus performer for decades, I've learned how to save kids from losing their innocence and their ability to dream. Imagination is the preview of life's coming attractions."

Flynn smiled at Albert, who then nudged him toward Rena. She was lost in her own thoughts. Flynn walked over to her, and they stood in silence looking over the calm lake. They watched Cordelia dive in and out of the water like swordfish playing. Flynn wondered if he would ever see Cordelia again, and if she could find it in her heart to forgive him.

Rena broke the silence by saying, "Let's go home."

"OK," Flynn said. "But I need to say good-bye."

Flynn said his good-byes to the performers, but when he got to Marcel, he seemed reluctant to talk to Flynn.

"Hey," Flynn said, trying to mend things. "I know you don't like me, but thanks for helping."

"I did it for Cordelia." Marcel stuck out his chest and crossed his arms. He had a look of pride on his face.

"I know," Flynn said, acknowledging Marcel's motives. "You did the right thing. Show her your good side; she'll warm up to you. It might help if you apologized to her."

"Apologize? For what?" Marcel was clearly unaware that he had done anything wrong to Cordelia.

"She told me about the time you tried to kiss her." Flynn said in a hushed tone. He didn't want to embarrass Marcel in front of the others.

Marcel bowed his head and whispered, "What did she say?"

"She originally had warm feelings toward you, but you came on too strong. I know you're supposed to be the tough guy during the circus performance, but Cordelia was turned off by that behavior the first time you were alone together. If you play your cards right, though, she might warm up to you again."

Marcel furrowed his brow. It looked to Flynn as if his advice might've sunken into Marcel's big head.

"Yeah," Marcel finally uttered after a few moments. "Maybe you're right. I let my circus character take over my personality."

Flynn extended his hand, and after some hesitation, Marcel shook his tiny hand. Marcel's strong handshake almost caused Flynn to buckle to the ground.

"Easy, big guy," Flynn joked. "Don't rip my arm off."

Marcel chuckled and let go of Flynn's hand.

Maybe Marcel isn't such a bad guy after all, Flynn thought.

Albert came up to Flynn and gave him a hug.

"When we get settled, I'll get in touch," Albert said.

"I'd like that," Flynn responded, feeling good inside.

"I'm sure things will work out with your parents," Albert reassured him. "Just show them the same level of passion for art as you've shown me the last few days."

"I will," Flynn said sincerely. "Well, I'm going walk Rena back to the motel. I hope we meet again."

"I'm sure we will," Albert said with certainty. "Goodbye, Flynn."

"Goodbye," Flynn said, a hint of sadness in his voice.

Cordelia stuck her head above the water and Flynn waved good-bye. She turned her back to him and dove back into the water, flipping her tail defiantly and making a big splash.

Flynn realized he couldn't change her feelings tonight, no matter how hard he tried. She might let go of her anger someday, but that would be up to her. *You can chew yourself up inside worrying about what others think...or might think*, Flynn realized.

Rena and Flynn stood at the edge of the woods with the placid lake behind them. Overhead, stars sparkled and stray clouds drifted by. A warm breeze blew through the trees, causing them to whisper calming thoughts, although their words were too low to be heard.

Flynn felt a sense of accomplishment; he had faced and overcome challenges. He had acted decisively and taken risks. Looking back, his actions weren't perfect; but things were better than they would've been if he had curled up in a ball and hidden under his blanket. He had exposed his real self to Rena, and she didn't think he was stupid. His fear of making mistakes or being rejected had caused him to lack confidence.

"Can I ask a silly question?" Flynn inquired, feeling pressure to clarify things.

"Sure," Rena replied, returning from her own deep thoughts.

"Why do you like me?" Flynn blurted out.

Rena hadn't expected such a direct and personal question. She knew she cared about Flynn, but why? What drew her toward him?

19

~

"Do you remember the showcase cabinet outside the art room at school?" Rena asked.

"Yeah," Flynn said.

"Every time Miss Hopper puts one of your drawings in the showcase, I'll stop and look at it. You're a great artist."

Rena's answer surprised Flynn. "Wow...Thank you." Flynn smiled. It was a positive response even though it didn't answer all the questions his heart was asking. "I've been checking you out too."

"Really?" She giggled.

"I mean, I've been checking out your artwork," he said, blushing.

"Freudian slip," she joked, winking at him.

"What I meant to say is I've been attracted to you too, a lot, but I had trouble getting to know you. I was so afraid I'd say something stupid that I would freeze up."

His words were clearer than his thoughts. He had exposed his heart and taken a risk by being honest. If he went too far, he knew his heart would be crushed and scarred forever. He held his breath and his heart stopped as he awaited a response.

Rena had been attracted to Flynn, and his art was at the root of it. It was the window through which she saw something valuable in him - something his awkwardness couldn't hide. It only took a few seconds to decide what to say, but it seemed like hours to each of them.

"I can't put my finger on it, but I've cared about you for a long time," Rena said, looking intently in Flynn's blue eyes. "I guess time will tell us what happens next."

"I look forward to the future," Flynn said with great relief. His heart was exploding. However things turned out, he and Rena were connected in a way that enabled them to be themselves around each other. The world felt perfect, but not for long.

The silence of the forest was disrupted by the faint sound of a helicopter.

"It must be the police making another pass," Flynn said.

"We should get going," Rena said, giving Flynn a worried look. "I need to get back to the motel before my mom goes crazy worrying about me."

At that moment, Paula and Rego walked over to Rena and Flynn.

"Do you guys need a ride?" Rego offered. "Paula and I can take you back to the motel. It would be a lot quicker."

"That would be great," Flynn said, graciously accepting their offer.

"Do you have a car to take us back to the motel?" Rena asked Rego. She didn't know about Paula and Rego's powers.

"No, we have something better." Paula jumped into the conversation.

White wings sprouted from Paula's and Rego's shoulder blades. White feathers spread out and began to flap like the wings of giant eagle.

"Wow." Rena's jaw dropped. "You guys can fly?"

"Can't all trapeze artists fly?" Paula asked coyly.

Rego wrapped his arms around Flynn's chest and Paula grabbed Rena's waist. Catching a breeze, they ascended over the lake and into the sky. Flynn looked down one last time and saw Cordelia lift her head out of the lake. Water dripped off her long hair, droplets landing on her shoulders. Silently, she watched Flynn fly into the night sky and out of her life.

Late Wednesday evening…
Flynn knocked on the door to Rena's room. No one answered, so he looked at Rena and shrugged his shoulders. They were confused because

their parents' cars were in the motel parking lot. Quietly, they stepped over to the next room.

Flynn's stomach grumbled as he knocked on the door; he hoped his dad had bought pizza to fill his aching belly.

"I bet the food is cold," Flynn whispered to Rena.

The door swung open.

"Come in," Detective Winslow commanded in an official-sounding voice. "We've been expecting you."

Rena and Flynn were shocked when they saw the detective answer the door. They obediently walked in and were greeted by angry stares from their parents.

"Where have you been?" Georgia asked, sounding both relieved and concerned.

"We've been worried sick." Flynn's father said angrily. "You better have a good explanation."

"It's a long story," Flynn said without elaborating. Besides, he didn't even know where to begin, or how much to say. Somehow in the frenzy of the evening, he hadn't thought about anything other than saving Albert and Cordelia. It now dawned on him that he and Rena could be in serious trouble.

"A long story?" Detective Winslow asked. "It better be a good one. I have to take you down to the Grand River Police Headquarters. This is their jurisdiction and their investigation."

"What are you saying?" Mrs. Gainsborough cried. "I'm sure they can explain everything. Give them a chance."

"Laws were broken tonight. I have no choice," the detective said firmly.

"Are you arresting them?" Mr. Gainsborough asked, concerned.

"That depends on the facts that turn up and how much Rena and your son cooperate," Detective Winslow stated.

Everyone gasped as Winslow reached under his jacket and pulled out two sets of handcuffs.

"This probably isn't necessary," he said as he cuffed Flynn's hands behind his back and then Rena's. "But I can't have them try and run away again."

The detective put his hands on their shoulders and escorted them out the door. Flynn smelled the pizza and knew he was going to miss dinner. That didn't matter, though, because his stomach was tied in knots and he felt nauseous as the detective guided him and Rena out of the motel and into an unmarked police car. As Flynn and Rena climbed silently into the back seat, they watched their parents jump into Ray's car and follow them to the police station.

Detective Winslow made a radio call to police headquarters and said, "I have the suspects in custody. I'm bringing them in, so be ready."

"OK, Roger that," squawked the radio.

The words echoed inside Flynn's head: *suspects, in custody, and bringing them in. This is unreal* Flynn thought. *Unfortunately this is real. Everything changed since I followed Rena into that circus tent. How could a quick decision make such a huge impact on my life and Rena's life too?*

Rena squirmed and shivered in the backseat. She fought back tears and made quick glances at Flynn. Since the detective might be listening to their conversation, she didn't know what to say.

Flynn bit his lip, hoping he would wake up safe inside his own bed. Sadly, he wasn't having a nightmare. He had to convince Detective Winslow he had saved innocent lives despite the stubborn facts. There was the jailbreak, sneaking Albert from the hospital, an assault on the police officers by Paula and Rego. And all the damage Marcel had done to the jail and cars. Even if he did tell his story, Flynn didn't want to reveal the whereabouts of his circus friends. No one could confirm his fantastic story without jeopardizing their own freedom. Flynn pushed away his feelings of panic; instead, he focused on the big picture.

Just tell the truth kept ringing in his ears, even though the truth was unbelievable. He wouldn't get beyond the rope freezing in mid-air before they would haul him away in a straitjacket. He didn't even believe his own story, so how could he convince the police his story was true?

❧

Detective Winslow parked in a reserved spot in front of the police station. Ray parked in a visitor's space. Winslow helped Flynn and Rena out of the car and then led them to the front door where a uniformed officer waited for them. Flynn and Rena's parents followed them into the building. Everyone remained silent as they followed the officer down a long corridor with monochrome walls and a checkered gray tile floor. After passing a few doors, the officer stopped and opened the door to a conference room. It had no windows, only a large mirror on the back wall. Detective Cassatt sat at a long table with a microphone on it. She held a notebook in one hand and a pen in the other. After everyone entered the room, the uniformed officer closed the door behind him.

"Sit down," Detective Cassatt requested coldly as she pointed to a few empty chairs.

Detective Winslow removed the handcuffs from Flynn and Rena and took a seat beside Detective Cassatt. Rena and Flynn rubbed their wrists and wiggled their shoulders, shaking off their discomfort. They sat down next to their parents, across the table from the detectives.

Before anyone could speak, Detective Cassatt stood up, placed her hands on her hips, and said, "You have the right to remain silent. Anything you say may be used against you in a court of law. You have the right to an attorney...."

Flynn's mind didn't absorb the rest of his Miranda Rights even though he had heard it many times at the movies and on TV. *Should I ask for a lawyer?* Flynn thought.

His parents looked at each other in silence, unsure what to say.

"We need a few minutes to discuss this," Mr. Gainsborough spoke up.

"OK, you have five minutes," Detective Cassatt said sternly, looking at her watch.

As the detectives left the room, Flynn wondered, *Is the microphone turned on? What if they are watching behind the two-way mirror?* Flynn had tons of questions running through his mind.

"What are we going to do?" Georgia asked, her eyes moist with tears.

Before anyone could answer the question, the door burst open with a loud clatter. Rena and Flynn gasped in disbelief when the detectives re-entered the room with Albert!

20

"**Y**our lawyer is here," Detective Cassatt announced loudly as she briskly walked through the door.

"Lawyer?" Ray muttered under his breath. He looked at Flynn and whispered, "I didn't call any lawyer."

"Shhh." Flynn covered Ray's mouth with his hand. "I'll explain later."

"Sorry I took so long to get here," Albert apologized.

Dressed in a business suit and carrying a briefcase, Albert brushed past the detectives. His wavy brown hair flowed over his ears. Luckily the detectives didn't recognize Albert since he looked a lot younger.

"I'll need some time with my clients," Albert declared forcefully. "I want the microphone turned off, and I don't want anyone watching us through the mirror."

"Of course," Detective Cassatt replied.

After the detectives left the room, Ray asked in bewilderment, "What's going on? Who are you?"

"It's a looong story," Albert said as he sat down on the opposite side of the table.

"I'm sure it is," Ray said. "Give us the short version."

"OK, OK. I'm Albert DaVinci, owner of the circus. My son Salvatore kidnapped your son without my knowledge."

"What?" Ray stammered and stood up in disbelief. His chair almost fell backward. "You're not a lawyer? You're tangled up with the circus? Geez, we'll all be in jail before the end of night."

Flynn saw panic in his mother's eyes as she clung to Ray's arm.

"Relax," Albert said, trying to calm Ray's nerves.

"Easy for you to say," Ray said.

"Dad, calm down." Flynn said calmly. "Albert is here to help us." Flynn wanted to mend their relationship. "You need to have an open mind. A lot of crazy things happened at the circus."

"OK, I'll try," Ray said, crossing his arms. "What kind of trouble are you in?"

"We broke the ringmaster's daughter out of jail." Flynn put his faith in his dad. He hoped he wouldn't blow up again.

"Arrrgh." Ray could barely hold back his frustration.

"Rena, did Flynn put you up to this?" Mr. Gainsborough asked in disbelief.

Rena felt backed into a corner and explained, "Dad, I wanted to help Flynn because I care about him. His friends were in serious trouble."

"Oh honey…You can't risk your future for this boy." Mrs. Gainsborough's voice trailed off.

Ray paced the conference room floor. "Flynn! Why?"

"Albert's granddaughter Cordelia was sick, and the police weren't going to help her," Flynn pleaded, trying to justify his actions.

"Maybe not," Ray sighed. "But why is that your problem?"

Flynn explained his reasoning. "Salvatore ordered me to take the rhinoceros to the lake for water. So Marcel chained me to a rhino. When we got to the lake, I was pulled underwater. Cordelia is a very good swimmer and saved me from drowning." Flynn held back a few details that would blow his father's mind.

"Flynn!" Ray looked stunned. "Why would you take a risk and break her out of jail. Now you could go to jail."

"I don't know." Flynn searched his feelings. "I guess I felt obligated. She saved my life, so I wanted to save her life." Flynn didn't want to tell his dad about Cordelia being a mermaid. He definitely wouldn't understand.

"What about him?" Ray demanded, pointing a finger at Albert. "Did you help him escape too?"

"Yes," Flynn told the truth, not holding back any more information.

"I hope you have a good reason." Ray stopped pacing the floor and sternly looked at his son.

"Albert helped me escape from the circus," Flynn replied and gulped.

"How?" Ray looked unsatisfied. "Rena is the one who told the police where you were."

"Yes." Flynn didn't argue with his point. "But do you know how she found me?"

"Wellllll," Ray stammered. "No."

"This is where the story gets crazy," Flynn warned his parents. "I drew a picture of Rena and she appeared at the circus. That's when I asked her to go to the police."

Ray and Georgia looked at Flynn as if he were crazy. Mrs. Gainsborough shook her head in disbelief.

"What?" Ray had a look of doubt. "Flynn, I want to believe your story. But why are you lying to us now? How do you expect us to believe such nonsense?"

"Flynn, you don't need to lie to us," Georgia implored on the verge of tears.

"I'm not lying!" Flynn protested.

"I don't believe you," Ray denounced Flynn's story. No one believed him except Rena and Albert.

"Give me a minute," Flynn begged for more time. "I can prove it!"

Flynn pulled the magic pencil out his shirt pocket and looked at the broken end. He looked over at Albert. Albert opened his briefcase, pulled out a small pencil sharpener, and handed it to Flynn. Flynn sharpened the pencil and grabbed the detective's large notepad. He drew a violin on the pad and laid it down on the conference table.

"So." Ray looked unconvinced. "You drew a violin. Now what?"

After a few seconds, a small violin pushed through the surface of the paper. Ray's eyes widened and he took a few steps backward. Flynn concentrated on the sketch and the violin turned from a pencil gray to light brown. It looked just like the violin Ray played as a hobby.

"Oh...my...gosh!" Ray squeaked in a state of awe.

Everyone in the room remained speechless.

"Albert gave me these powers," Flynn explained to everyone. "If it wasn't for Albert, I would be Salvatore's prisoner forever. Albert saved me."

Ray sat down in a chair and stared at the violin. Flynn's artistic talent shocked everyone.

"Dad?" Flynn snapped his fingers. "Are you still with me?"

"Huh?" Ray needed time to process all the information.

"Do you still think I'm lying?" Flynn inquired.

"I'm not sure what to think." Ray shook his head in disbelief. "You left the house to think about your problems. You were kidnapped and given this incredible gift."

"Yep." Flynn agreed with the summary. "Cordelia and Albert's lives were in danger, so I used my powers to save them."

"Now, how do you explain that to a judge?" Ray posed a question.

Flynn didn't know the answer. "I guess I'll figure something out. I'm making up plans as I go along."

"Ha-ha." Ray laughed nervously. "But we need a real lawyer. Not a circus performer."

"I still have few tricks up my sleeve," Albert professed.

Albert got up and stood by the door. He paused and turned around. "OK, folks, I'm going to bring the police back in and talk to them. Until I tell you differently, don't answer any questions unless I ask them. Flynn hide the violin in the wasterbasket." Albert walked out the door.

The parents sat silently with stressed looks on their faces.

Ray leaned over and said to Flynn, "Albert better not make things worse..."

Flynn and Rena had plenty of things to worry about, but they didn't get too far down the list, because the door opened after just a few minutes.

Albert led the detectives back into the conference room and sat down at the table. Rena and Flynn were to Albert's right. Their parents sat to the left of Albert, and the detectives sat on the opposite side of the table.

"Could you tell me the status of the investigation?" Albert asked.

"Salvatore kept plenty of accounting records," Detective Cassatt replied. "We know who he stole from and what he took. We'll be contacting the victims and returning the money and jewelry."

Flynn let out a small sigh of relief. *Rena's parents will get back their money and my dad won't lose his job or his paycheck.*

"Wait a minute." Mr. Gainsborough's face lit up. "Are you saying we were robbed at the circus the other night? How did this happen? I don't remember!"

"Yes, Mr. Gainsborough. We found your wife's jewelry in Salvatore's motor home." Detective Cassatt continued, "I don't know why you or the other victims don't remember being robbed. Also, we aren't sure who else is involved in the theft. We suspect others were helping Salvatore, probably Jack with the lions and the big guy with the muscles. What's his name?"

"Marcel," Flynn added, realizing after the fact that he should just keep his mouth shut and let Albert do the talking.

"That's right," Cassatt said, raising her eyebrows at Flynn. "Marcel. We have no idea what happened to him, which leads me to your clients. We believe Marcel and your clients freed Albert and Cordelia. The stories we received from the policemen at the scene are a bit confusing, and, well, hard to believe. I'm still trying to put the pieces together."

"Why do you think my clients were involved?" Albert asked intently.

"Security cameras show two people who look like Flynn and Rena at the police station and hospital," Cassatt replied. "Fingerprints should confirm my hunch. If that's true, I'm afraid they'll no longer be considered innocent victims. That's why I need to ask them questions. It's critical to getting a fair outcome. I presume as their lawyer you'll advise them to cooperate to clear their names."

As the detective talked, Albert opened his briefcase and fiddled with something inside it. The lid blocked the detective's line of sight, and she and the other detective couldn't see Albert's hands.

"Would that be OK?" Detective Winslow spoke up. "Can we ask your clients a few questions about what happened?"

"Ahhhh, I think I can provide you with all the answers you will need…." Albert's voice trailed off as he pulled out his crystal ball from inside the briefcase and placed it on the conference table.

Winslow looked at Detective Cassatt and shrugged his shoulders in disbelief.

"I'm not sure what's going on, but this is a serious matter," Detective Cassatt said, appearing agitated.

"Have you heard of the butterfly effect?" Albert asked in all seriousness.

"I think so," Detective Winslow said, a perplexed look on his face.

Suddenly, a swarm of brightly colored butterflies flew out of the open briefcase and filled the room. Everyone looked around in total shock. A bright flash of light emitted from the crystal ball. Everyone covered their eyes for a moment, and then the light slowly dimmed.

"If a butterfly flaps its wings on one side of the earth, it may cause a hurricane on the other side of the earth. It's a ripple effect that causes changes to the future."

"What are you talking about?" Detective Cassatt shook her head in confusion.

"Watch the crystal ball," Albert instructed. "It will answer all your questions."

Everyone silently stared at the crystal ball. They were baffled when the core glowed bright amber followed by swirling purple smoke.

"What the heck is going on?" Detective Winslow asked barely above a whisper.

A blurry image slowly came into focus. Like a tiny movie screen, scenes from the last few days played inside the sphere. First it showed the lions ready to attack Deana. Then it showed Salvatore asking for money in exchange for her safety and hypnotizing Rena's parents.

Mr. Gainsborough looked at Albert and whispered, "So that's why I don't remember."

Albert nodded.

The next scene showed Salvatore kidnapping Flynn. The crystal ball provided all the evidence the detectives needed for their investigation.

It revealed that the true villains were Salvatore and Jack. Everyone else was basically innocent.

"But what about all the damage done to the prison and the cars?" Detective Cassatt asked, needing more information. "Who's responsible for that?"

"One moment," Albert said in a calm and soothing voice.

The image flickered, like the movie reel was changing. The crystal ball fast-forwarded and showed Flynn concerned about Albert and Cordelia almost dying. It showed Flynn, with some help, rescuing them.

"See?" Detective Cassatt interjected. "I knew Rena and Flynn were there."

"But there's more," Albert said somberly.

The crystal ball kept playing past the evening and showed everyone the future. It showed a future where the police arrested Flynn and Rena tonight. They saw how their lives and futures would be ruined after their arrest. Flynn wouldn't make it to college and couldn't find a job. Rena would struggle with school and eventually drop out. The image blurred and faded inside a purple swirl.

"But the future doesn't have to look like this." Albert raised his eyebrows, his eyes glowing with a sense of hope. "We can change the future tonight."

Albert rubbed his hands over the crystal ball, closed his eyes, and bowed his head. He mumbled some words under his breath that no one, not even Flynn, could hear.

The purple swirled counterclockwise and stopped. The image faded in and a new film started to play. It showed the police releasing Flynn and Rena into the custody of their parents. They were given a warning since they had never been in trouble with the law before. They saw Marcel making restitution by paying for the cars he had wrecked and Salvatore and Jack going to prison for their crimes. It also showed Flynn and Rena both finishing high school and college.

There was a long pause as the detectives took in all the information.

"Could you give us a minute while I speak with my boss?" Detective Cassatt asked.

"Certainly," Albert said confidently.

After the detectives left the room, Albert fumbled through his brief-case until he found the poster Flynn had created to promote the circus. Albert handed the poster to Flynn.

"Keep this. You'll need it someday."

"OK," Flynn responded, a bit confused and then he asked in a whisper, "Can your crystal ball really see the future?"

"Think of it this way Flynn," Albert said in a hushed tone. "Your life can take multiple paths along your journey. Use your mind like a crystal ball and choose your path wisely," he said with a wink and a smile.

After several minutes, the detectives returned. Flynn couldn't read their stern and unflinching facial expressions. They sat down opposite Flynn, Rena and their parents. Time ticked slowly as Flynn's heart beat faster.

Detective Cassatt cleared her throat and said, "I spoke with the chief of police and the prosecutor. I explained all the facts surrounding your story."

Flynn and Rena held their breaths. Georgia squeezed Ray's hand. Rena's parents wrapped their arms around her waist.

"We've decided to release Flynn and Rena to their parents. The prosecutor isn't going to press charges. Marcel will pay for the car repairs. The circus will be responsible if he doesn't."

"Can you stick around to go over the details?" Detective Winslow added, looking at Albert.

Albert exhaled deeply and patted Flynn on the head. He gave him a quick smile, then turned to the detectives and said, "Yes, I can wrap up any paperwork."

21

~

Late Wednesday night in Flynn's motel room...

Exhausted by the long day, Ray drove everyone back to the motel. Flynn and Rena were quiet even though they had a million thoughts running through their minds. Rena struggled to keep her eyes open, and she began to fall asleep. She rested her head on Flynn's shoulder.

When they arrived back at the motel, Flynn's parents were too tired to ask any more questions. All they wanted to do was sleep off the long day, so everyone trudged silently to their rooms.

"Goodnight." Georgia nodded at Mrs. Gainsborough as Ray swiped the room key in the door.

"Night," Mrs. Gainsborough said as she yawned and entered her room.

Flynn took a long gaze at Rena as she shuffled into the motel room. She had her head bowed, exposing the arc of her neckline. The subtle curve, smooth skin, and jawline made a beautiful silhouette, something he could draw over and over again.

~

Flynn ignored the cold pizza, undressed down to his boxer shorts, and crawled into bed. His eyelids grew heavy and he quickly fell asleep.

After a few hours, he woke to the sound of footsteps. When his eyelids flipped open, he saw Salvatore standing over him! Salvatore snapped

Flynn's magic pencil into two pieces. He threw the pencil on the floor and wrapped his callous hands around Flynn's neck. Unable to make a sound, Flynn frantically tried to pry Salvatore's hands free and kicked at Salvatore with his knees.

"You destroyed my circus and my life." Salvatore snarled. His face twisted in rage and insanity. "Then you divided my family. Before I kill you, tell me where my daughter is!"

The weight of Salvatore's body almost crushed Flynn's windpipe. He gasped for air as his heart pounded against his rib cage. Flynn's face began turning blue.

Before he passed out, Flynn muttered, "I...will...never...tell... you."

"Fine, you little brat!" Salvatore spat with fury in his eyes. "You want to be brave? Meet your fate!"

He squeezed Flynn's neck until he could no longer breathe. As Flynn's life flashed before his eyes, Salvatore's face began to melt, bend, and warp into Flynn's father's face. He couldn't believe what he was seeing. He let out a scream, but his father's grip tightened.

Suddenly, Flynn heard his father's voice. "Wake-up!"

He sprung out of bed. His blanket was wrapped around his neck, his pillow was on the floor, and the bed sheets were soaked with sweat.

It was only a nightmare. Flynn sighed, catching his breath. He untangled the blanket, picked up his pillow, and fell back asleep still panting.

The sunlight shining through the motel window woke Flynn up the next morning. Ray sat at a table, reading the newspaper. Georgia sat in front of a mirror doing her make-up.

"Good morning," Ray said, laying down the paper. "Are you OK?" Ray's tone sounded sincere.

Maybe he's trying to make up for the last few days. Flynn thought.

"I had a nightmare," Flynn announced as he sat across the table from his father. "But I think I'm going to be OK."

"Good, good. You'll work through it," Ray said as he folded his arms and stared intently at Flynn.

"What's wrong?" he asked with genuine concern. "Why did you run away from home?"

"I wasn't trying to run away," Flynn explained. "I went for a bike ride to sort things out in my head."

Georgia stopped applying her make-up and turned around and asked, "What were you trying to sort out?"

"A lot of things. It feels like I have no control over my future. I don't think people see the real me, and I'm afraid to be myself. I had a bad day at school, and when I got home, I felt I couldn't talk about my feelings. Terrible things happened at the circus, but they helped me realize I need to take charge of my life. I want to study art in college, but I didn't know how to talk to you about it."

"We've been over this," Ray tried to restrain his temper. "Your mother and I don't think you can make a living at art. We want you to succeed in life."

"We want what is best for you and your future," Georgia added.

"What about happiness?" Flynn countered. "Will I be happy following the life you choose for me?"

"Flynn, it's complicated." Ray paused. "Of course we want you to be happy. When I was a teenager, I loved playing the violin. I played it when I should've been studying or saving money for college. I didn't know if I was good enough to make a living at it. I'll never know because I didn't go after it with my whole heart. Like music, art is a risky career. So instead, I encouraged you to find a more secure career."

Flynn listened in silence, taking in all of his father's words.

"And," Ray continued, "I'm not sure if I can afford an expensive art college." Ray had tears in his eyes. He had never been so honest with Flynn, or himself for that matter.

"Mom, Dad," Flynn had a warm feeling in his chest. He could tell his parents were genuinely concerned about him. They weren't trying to punish him, but rather to protect him. "I'll graduate from high school in a couple of years. Then I'll be in college. When does my life belong to me?" Flynn asked with determination and then paused for a moment, "I want to take control of my life. No matter how things work out, I won't have anyone to blame but myself. I'll also get a summer job to earn money for college, and I will apply for scholarships. I'll work hard on other classes, just in case art doesn't work out."

Georgia looked at her husband. Ray unfolded his arms and stood up from the table, looking directly into Flynn's eyes. Flynn prepared himself for another argument. His father's eyes were firm and unflinching, but Ray simply placed his hand on Flynn's shoulder.

"I keep forgetting that you're turning into a man." Ray looked at his son differently. "Even though we have concerns with your decision, we'll respect your right to choose your path in life."

Georgia gave Flynn a hug and whispered in his ear, "Don't run away from us or your problems. Next time, let's talk about it."

"I'm sorry for the way I've been acting," Ray apologized humbly. "I love you, son."

"I love you too," Flynn replied.

They embraced for a moment, and then Flynn jumped in the shower and got ready to make the long drive home.

As they gathered their things and headed to the checkout counter, Georgia asked, "Should we go home or should I take Flynn to school?"

"Drop me off at home so I can get my work truck," Ray said. "It sounds like I still have a job, thanks to Flynn." Ray smiled and patted his son on the back.

Flynn beamed with pride and said, "Mom, I'll go to school. I want to see Rena."

"OK." Georgia let out a sigh of relief.

22

~

Earlier Thursday morning in Rena's motel room…

"Rena, honey. Wake up." Rena's mom tapped her on the shoulders. "You're going to be late for school."

Rena hadn't heard any alarm clock. She had been bundled up in a cozy blanket with her face buried in a pillow.

"What time is it?" Rena could barely open her sleepy eyes. "I need some caffeine."

"It's five thirty. Do you want to go to school?" Rena's mom saw the tired look in Rena's eyes. "You had a long day yesterday. I can call the school and tell them you're sick."

"No." Rena yawned. "I'll be fine after some coffee."

"The motel lobby should have some." Rena's mom smiled.

"OK," Rena yawned again.

Rena dragged her feet into the bathroom for a shower. Every few minutes, she turned the cold water on full blast. The sudden spray sent jolts through her body, making her feel more awake and alert. After the shower, she dried herself with a towel, got dressed, and followed her mother downstairs to the lobby. A hot cup of coffee was waiting for her. She sipped the coffee and grabbed a donut from a tray next to the coffee machine. She wondered if Flynn was still in his room since she didn't see him in the lobby.

While her parents went outside to start the car, Rena swallowed the rest of her coffee. She then headed to the parking lot where her parents were waiting. She saw Flynn's parents' car still in the parking lot.

Rena dozed off a few times as they traveled back to Whitehall. She wanted to talk to Flynn, but her parents had insisted on leaving early. *I guess I can talk to him at school*, Rena thought.

About an hour later, they arrived back in Whitehall. They stopped and picked up Deana from her grandparents' house. After that, Mr. Gainsborough dropped both girls off at school.

"Don't disappear with Flynn again," Rena's mom joked as Rena jumped out of the car.

"Ha-ha. Very funny," Rena said, playing innocent.

Deana and Rena arrived at school a few minutes before the opening bell. Rena headed straight for John's locker and tapped him on the shoulder.

"I have great news!" Rena glowed.

"Where have you been?" John asked with enthusiasm.

"Well, that's a long story." Rena beamed. "But, I found Flynn! He's coming home."

"Are you kidding me?" John said, relief washing over his face. He looked down the hall at Flynn's locker. "Where is he? I don't see him."

"He's probably still at the Grand River Motel with his parents," Rena explained.

"Grand River?" John didn't understand. "How did he get there?"

"He was kidnapped!" Rena exclaimed. "And the detectives are building a case against the kidnappers."

"No way!" John said, clearly shocked by the news. "I thought he ran away from his dad. Wow! Do you think he'll be back today?"

"I'm not sure," Rena said.

"Is he all right?" John asked, concerned for his friend.

"Yeah. But he has changed."

"What do you mean changed?" John asked, his eyes narrowing slightly.

"Well," Rena said and smiled because she knew Flynn's secret, "he can change his drawings into real objects."

"That's the craziest thing I've ever heard!" Deana interjected.

Deana had been standing behind Rena the whole time. Without an invitation, she jumped into Rena and John's conversation.

"I always knew you were a little strange, but now you are a liar too." Deana wagged her finger at Rena.

"I'm not lying. It's true." Rena's blood boiled as she defended herself.

I should've talked to John in private, Rena thought about her actions with regret. *Now my sister is going to tell the whole school.*

"Whatever. They should put you and Flynn in a loony bin." Deana crossed her arms and mocked Rena.

"I'm not crazy!" Rena clenched her teeth and her face turned red.

Deana stuck up her nose, held up her hand, and walked away.

"Why are you such a jerk?" Rena muttered under her breath.

"I believe you," John said, placing his hand on Rena's shoulder.

"Thanks," Rena replied.

The bell rang and Rena ran to math class and sat in the back of the room. Mr. Hawkings wrote formulas on the board. Instead of numbers, though, Rena saw music notes. They strung together and formed an original music composition. She rubbed her sleepy eyes and felt tired again. Soon her eyes closed and she fell asleep.

"Rena!" Mr. Hawkings yelled. "Wake up!"

Students giggled as she straightened up in her seat. *I'm not the only one who falls asleep in math*, she thought.

"Sorry, Mr. Hawkings," Rena apologized, trying to avoid detention. "I didn't get a lot of sleep last night."

"Don't let it happen again," Mr. Hawkings warned.

Rena fought to keep her eyes open for the rest of the period. Her ears perked up when she heard the bell ring. She ran to her locker, dropped off her math textbook, and picked up her drumsticks. She followed her fellow band mates to class. She took her spot next to her drums as the other students grabbed their instruments from their band lockers.

After the students finished tuning up their instruments, Mr. Anders announced, "We're going to practice 'Circus Overture' by William Schuman today. Rena, I want you to do the timpani solo. Are you ready? Have you been practicing?"

"Yes, Mr. Anders." Rena nodded. "I think I'm ready."

"Let's hope so," Mr. Anders remarked.

The class skillfully played the overture while Rena patiently waited for her solo. Mr. Anders looked over at Rena. She took a deep breath and closed her eyes, letting the music flow though her mind. At first, she followed the beat, but before she realized what she was doing, she began playing something else, something new that came to her in the moment. She expanded on the solo, making it her own melody. A few of her band members joined in, but eventually fell off as Rena had gone beyond them.

She snapped back to reality when she finished. She looked around and saw the whole class, including Mr. Anders, staring at her with their mouths wide open. The band teacher quietly set his conductor's stick down on his music stand.

Oh no, Rena thought. *I'm in trouble again.* She waited nervously while everyone stayed quiet. *I wish someone would say something*, she impatiently thought.

Mr. Anders clapped his hands and announced, "Rena, that was wonderful. Wow! I didn't see that coming."

Rena smiled at his compliment. Her musical gift allowed music to flow naturally. Ruben scowled; he would now need to find someone else to pick on in band class.

Mr. Anders had them practice the music a few more times. Each time they played it, Rena got better and better as she learned to play more naturally. Forty minutes later, the bell rang signaling that the students put away their instruments. Rena looked up from her drums and saw Mr. Anders smile with approval. She didn't know it then, but he would give her many more compliments as she continued to impress people with her musical talent.

As she went to put away her drumsticks, she wondered where Flynn was. The day felt as if it was dragging on and on as she waited for his return.

23

After stopping at Nighthawk's Cafe for breakfast and dropping Ray off at home, Georgia drove Flynn to school. They had a rough seventy-two hours, but Georgia didn't want Flynn to miss the last few classes of the day. He felt a little nervous about going back to school, but not as much as before he was kidnapped.

Georgia got out car and gave Flynn a hug.

"Don't forget your backpack," she reminded her son, reaching into the back seat.

As Flynn strolled down the sidewalk, Georgia shouted out the car window, "Hurry up! You've missed enough school the last few days."

"OK," Flynn shouted back. "See you in a few hours."

Flynn waved to his mom as he entered the front door of the high school. While heading to his locker, a few kids stopped talking. Suddenly, John ran up beside Flynn and put him in a headlock. Normally, this didn't bother Flynn, but he tried being confident in his own skin.

"Dude, knock it off." Flynn squirmed out of John's arms.

"What happened? How did you get away?" John let go and slapped him on the back.

"It's a long story." Flynn laughed. He knew he should keep quiet on most of the details.

"Rena and I looked everywhere for you." John expressed his concern. "And, um, I was worried about you."

"Really?" Flynn chuckled. "Give me a hug, you big softy."

Flynn stretched out his arms and pretended to give his friend a hug.

"What?" John pushed away his arms. "I'm not hugging you."

"I know." Flynn laughed. "I was just messing with you."

When they got to English class, the room fell silent; everyone turned to look at Flynn. *What the heck is going on? Everyone is acting really strange,* Flynn thought.

Mr. Blake pulled Flynn aside before he went to his desk.

"I'm glad you're back," Mr. Blake whispered.

"Thanks." Flynn responded.

"You don't need to read in front of the class," Mr. Blake said, trying to be thoughtful. "I know you haven't had time to practice reading in front of your parents."

"No, it's OK. I can do it," Flynn replied.

Some students whispered among themselves as Flynn took his seat. Flynn shook his head when he heard Ruben whisper, "Flynn is going to jail because he ran away from home and he tried to kill someone."

"No, fool," Vinnie mumbled. "He ran away because his parents are crazy."

Flynn heard muffled laughter. *Where do they come up with these crazy rumors?* he wondered.

One comment, however, shocked Flynn. He heard Ruben say, "Where did Deana get her outfit, the Salvation Army?"

Flynn looked at Deana. She wasn't wearing any of her designer clothes; she was wearing Rena clothes.

Mr. Blake abruptly said, "OK, quiet down and quit wasting time." Pointing a finger at Flynn, he said, "Can you starting reading Chapter Twenty-Five on page two hundred and eleven in *The Catcher in the Rye?*"

"Sure," Flynn replied. He flipped open the book and confidently read the passage: "The thing with kids is, if they want to grab for the gold ring, you have to let them do it, and not say anything. If they fall off, they fall off, but it's bad if you say anything to them."

Flynn went on to read flawlessly for the next several minutes.

"Good job!" Mr. Blake announced with a smile when Flynn was finished reading.

"What happened to sta-ta-ta-ta-tutter boy?" Vinnie stirred up the class. "Someone kidnapped the real Flynn."

The class broke into laughter.

"That's it," Mr. Blake said. "Forget practice! You have detention."

"Coach!" Vinnie pleaded, trying to make amends. "I was just kidding."

"Who's next to read?" Mr. Blake ignored Vinnie's pleas.

"But, Coach!" Vinnie whined remorsefully.

"Zip it." It was clear that Mr. Blake wasn't going to argue.

The hour flew by, and everyone rushed for the door when the bell rang.

Flynn and John stepped into the hallway, and a group of students cornered them like bees to a hive.

"Where have you been?" Vinnie asked.

"Rena said your drawings turn into real objects." Deana ridiculed him. "Can you draw me a million dollars?"

The group of students laughed at Deana's silly question. Flynn felt overwhelmed by his new celebrity status.

BBBRRRIIIIIING!

Saved by the warning bell, Flynn drew a deep breath and fired back at the crowd. "Are you that gullible to think I got arrested and I have a magic pencil that can turn drawings into real objects?"

Everyone grew silent as they looked at Flynn. They must've expected him to wander off with his tail between his legs.

"And, Deana, if I had the ability to draw real money, why would I come back to school?" Flynn asked.

Flynn's classmates fell silent when he finally stood up to them. They appeared to be shocked by his newfound confidence. They stepped aside while Flynn and John walked down the hall toward art class.

"Geez," John commented. "That was crazy."

"Yeah," Flynn agreed. "Why did Rena rat me out?"

"She didn't," John said. "Deana overheard me and Rena's conversation."

"Oh, OK," Flynn replied, relaxing a little bit.

Miss Hopper jumped out of her seat and smiled when Flynn entered the room.

"What happened?" Miss Hopper asked.

"It's a long story," Flynn said, already tired of explaining himself.

"Are you OK?" she asked with concern.

"Yeah," Flynn replied. "I hate to say it, but I missed school and home."

"I'm just happy you're back," she assured him.

"Me too!" Flynn exclaimed as he walked to his seat in the back of the class.

Over his shoulder, he overheard Miss Hopper say, "Are you ready to give your art report today?"

When is she going to give me a break? Flynn wondered with amusement. *I'm back five minutes and she wants my report.*

Then Flynn remembered Albert's parting gift - the poster he created for the circus. *How did Albert know I was going to need the poster for my art report? Oh, yeah, he has the crystal ball; he can see everything. I wonder if he knew all along things would work out for the circus and for me?* Flynn reached into his backpack and grabbed the poster he had drawn.

"Yes, I'm ready," he responded.

He walked up to the front of the class, and taped the poster on the white board.

"The name of my report is 'Traveling Circus,'" Flynn stated in a clear voice.

Oh boy, this is going to be good, Rena smiled.

The drawing had Cordelia lying on top of the rhinoceros and holding up a rabbit. Salvatore stood in front of the rhinoceros, holding a pocket watch. Standing next to Salvatore was the lioness, and a white swan flew in the sky.

Flynn gave his best analysis of the drawing. "The rhinoceros looks to our future, which is death. The brave lioness is looking at the past. The mermaid enjoys the present moment, the rabbit represents insecurity and the man holding a pocket watch symbolizes our memories. The swan symbolizes how fast life and beauty fly by us."

"I don't recognize that picture," Miss Hopper said, interrupting his report. "Who's the artist that created the drawing?"

"I did the report on me," Flynn boldly answered. "I drew it."

His boldness caused murmuring among the class.

"You were supposed to do report on a famous artist, Flynn," she said, a look of disappointment on her face.

"I will be a famous artist one day," Flynn responded.

Everyone but Rena and John laughed at Flynn's response. He squared his shoulders, stood up straight, and walked back to his seat.

"Well," Miss Hopper said reluctantly, "I'm going to deduct points since you didn't follow my directions exactly."

Flynn no longer worried about criticism; he had made a decision and stuck to it, knowing there might be consequences for his bold actions.

John leaned over and whispered, "Your picture is great. Miss Hopper didn't say you couldn't do the report on yourself. She never said how famous."

Flynn looked across the room and saw Rena smiling at him. Her friend whispered in her ear and she blushed.

"By the way, she likes you." John spoke out the side of his mouth.

"Yeah," Flynn agreed quietly. "I kinda figured that out."

"Did you kiss her yet?" John prodded Flynn.

"Nooo." Flynn had his own timeline for things. "Not yet, but it's going to happen."

"Better hurry up." John warned. "She's not going to wait around forever."

Miss Hopper talked about the next assignment for the rest of the hour. When the bell rang, Flynn stopped Rena before she left.

"Rena, do you have a minute?" Flynn mustered up all his courage. Even though he was back in his old environment, he felt determined to go after what's important to him.

"Sure." Rena stopped walking while her friends continued out of the classroom.

"I haven't forgotten my promise." Flynn smiled.

"Oh yeah?" Rena asked, slightly puzzled.

"I wanted to give you a drawing for putting your faith in me," Flynn said.

He dug inside his backpack for his magic pencil, but all he found was a regular one. He looked at it for a second and then grabbed a sketchpad. He quickly drew a picture for her. Using the power of imagination, the drawing slowly lifted off the paper and became a real object. At that moment, he realized that creativity was within him, not the pencil. As if there were an invisible paintbrush, the drawing turned from charcoal to color. The stem and leaves filled with green, and the petals bloomed red. He plucked the flower from the paper, smiled, and handed the rose to Rena. Her cheeks blushed the color of the petals.

The End

New Book Coming Soon!

Traveling Circus
And the Secret Talent Scroll

The prequel follows the adventures of Cordelia
as she discovers the mystery behind the
Secret Talent Scroll!